Decline & Fall of Macready's Club

A dystopian fable told by a gentleman

Paperback Edition First Publishing in Great Britain in 2024
by aSys Publishing

eBook Edition First Publishing in Great Britain in 2024
by aSys Publishing

Copyright © a gentleman

The author has asserted his rights under 'the Copyright
Designs and Patents Act 1988'

No part of this document may be reproduced or
transmitted in any form or by any means, electronic,
mechanical, photocopying, recording, or otherwise, without
prior written permission of Author.

aSys Publishing

Paperback ISBN: 978-1-913438-83-8
Hardback ISBN: 978-1-913438-85-2

http://www.asys-publishing.co.uk

Disclaimer

This is a work of fiction that draws loosely on certain real events for the purposes of satire and nothing else. Names, characters, events, and incidents are products of the author's imagination and are used in the pursuit of humour only. Any resemblance to actual persons, living or dead, is unintended and coincidental.

To my dearest sister, who was often a guest at my club. She loved coming there, but told me (in no uncertain terms) that if we changed the rules to admit women as members, she would rather I took her to a decent restaurant.

Cartoons by Mike Mosedale

Images of Macready are licensed by the National Portrait Gallery

The row of London houses on the title page is licensed by Shutterstock

William Macready

William Macready was a famous actor, and when he died in 1873 a club was inaugurated in his honour which was to become even more famous than he:

Macready's Club

Part One

1 The Problem

The avowed purpose of Macready's Club was to promote the arts, with particular emphasis on the theatre; and by the end of the 19th century, every prominent actor in Britain had joined. Hot on the heels of the feet that trod the boards came playwrights, politicians, judges, barristers, and even solicitors. Renowned musicians were keen to join Macready's: composers, conductors, performers. A much-loved star of the music hall joined in 1911 and sang at the club's Christmas festivities every year until a German bomb landed on his house in 1943 and killed him and everyone else living there.

Post-war television created no end of famous faces wanting to join Macready's, and it wasn't long before these too were popping up in the coffee room like overnight mushrooms, along with captains of industry and (much-higher ranking) representatives of the armed forces. So popular did Macready's become, that by the time of its grand centenary celebrations in 1973, the cap on members being one thousand and the mortality rate among them being irritatingly slow, it was rumoured that there was a ten-year wait between proposal and election.

Some said it was at the centenary dinner that Macready's lustre began to tarnish. The guest of honour was an actress and Dame of the British Empire who had recently won an Oscar. The then chairman proclaimed in a reckless after-dinner speech that he looked forward to the day when he could welcome her, not as a guest but as a member. Audible gasps and a shouted "sit down!" were challenged by a ripple of supportive applause and a loud "hear, hear".

Whether his flush-faced enthusiasm started it all, or whether the fabric of Macready's had already begun to crumble with no help from the chairman, by the early 2020s the club was in serious decline, subject to sustained criticism and mockery, because its woefully out-of-date 19th century rules did not allow women to join, and a recent poll of members—leaked to the press by unscrupulous reformers—had decided by a slim majority to keep it that way.

The vote to preserve the status quo precipitated a squall of resignations, headed by a certain Lord Pugh (his detractors pronounced it "Puff"). His letter to the secretary, posted on the club notice board, said:

> *"I am unable, in all conscience, to remain a member of a club which discriminates against women."*

Someone pinned a hand-written note underneath it:

> *"Curious that that same conscience didn't balk at some of the things he did as Home Secretary."*

The note was taken down, but not before it had been read by half the club. In an email circulated to the entire membership, the chairman made a veiled reference to the note and reminded everyone of the ethos of Macready's and "good fellowship". The note went up again.

And so it was that acrimony entered what had previously been a civilised, if sometimes heated, debate. Two rival camps emerged, each claiming the certainty of Macready's allegiance had he still been alive—"*It's what Macready would have wanted*" versus "*Macready would be turning in his grav*e".

Those resisting change were called misogynist by the reforming camp; and the reformers were called 'woke' by the status quo camp. Each faction complained bitterly that the other was engaged in highly organised canvassing, contrary to the conventions of the club; while at the same time each faction busily proselytised as many members as possible to 'do the right thing'.

At a particularly stormy AGM, and in spite of several *ad hominem* attacks on anyone who dared suggest that things were rather nice as they were, a motion to change the rules so as to permit the election of women members failed to reach the necessary two-thirds majority for a rule-change. But some 55% had voted in favour. And although the reformers claimed a moral victory, and the status quos claimed, "the only victory that matters", neither side felt they had won, and they barely acknowledged each other in the bar afterwards.

At the date on which this history begins, the club was heading towards another fractious extraordinary general meeting and yet another vote on whether to admit women as members.

*

"We're doomed," said Patrick. "It's like an Irish referendum: they'll keep on at it until they get the result they want."

Patrick Rowlands was an actor of the old school and his delivery of "doomed" was magnificent. Of medium height, a plump figure gave him the affectionate nickname 'Roly Poly'. He wore a tweed jacket and corduroy trousers, and with the wide stripes on his garish Macready tie ill-matched against a blue checked shirt, he was the very picture of a warm, avuncular, out-of-work actor.

"They have the ear of some wretched journalist at the Bugle," he said.

A passing member muttered "You don't read that rag, do you?"

"My attention is sometimes drawn to it," said Roly Poly, theatrically over-defensive.

"I read it," said Martin. "Online. There's a snide op-ed piece about us every other hour, peppered with information that could only come from someone on the inside. We have a mole, gentlemen."

His use of the words "us" and "we" was perhaps a little presumptuous. He was only a candidate for membership and was there as a guest. He had been abandoned by his host and remained in the bar under the protection of other members. He wore a short beard, a dingy dark suit, and a dog-collar. No one was certain which of the available Christian sects the dog-collar signified, or to what cathedral, church, or chapel Martin was attached. It might have been none. It was possible that the whole uniform was a sham.

Martin was a source of vicious gossip, clerical and civilian, holy and unholy. And because he was popular in the bar and his Macready acolytes found him amusing company, he had been allowed to creep closer than he should have to an enjoyment of the privileges of membership—perhaps in anticipation of what was widely regarded as certain election. Nobody (that is, nobody with whom these pages are concerned) could remember what his surname was. Martin was just "Martin".

"Whoever is leaking the club's business to the press should be sacked,'" said Hector, flushed with anger.

The Hon. Hector Floodgate was a raffish, extremely popular, enormously rich young member. His older brother inherited the viscountcy (which could be traced through a line of Floodgates back to a slave-trader in the 18th Century), as well as a bank, a Georgian pile in Yorkshire, and the vast estate that went with it. Hector, on the other hand, inherited a huge fortune from his late mother, who thought her favourite son was otherwise hard-done-by, as second sons so often are, and left him everything that she had been bequeathed by her billionaire American father. Hector was one of a few members who kept his own wine in the Macready cellars, and who drank champagne from an engraved silver tankard reserved for him behind the bar.

"There's no point in sacking him now," said Martin. "The damage was done months ago."

"But we mustn't give up without a fight," said James Purdey.

"Hear, hear," said Roly Poly. "Absolutely! Good man!"

Purdey was a barrister, recently appointed the youngest King's Counsel on record—something he occasionally let slip. He liked to foster his courtroom reputation as a 'fighter': "*both barrels, right and left*" was his routine boast after a victory, with a mime and vocal effects to accompany it. Testimonials in the legal directories spoke of James Purdey KC as "n*ot afraid of a scrap*". (Unkind rumour had it that he wrote them himself, pretending to be a client.) His resistance to women membership was at odds with the position taken by most other KCs ('silks') in Macready's, who tended to support the "*let 'em in*" camp.

Hugger-mugger with a left-wing theatre director and a couple of BBC journalists the other end of the long bar, were three such "*let 'em in*" silks. One of them was a highly-paid commercial silk. Another was an MP who hadn't conducted any litigation worthy the name other than his own disastrous divorce. The last of them was a criminal defence barrister in a shiny suit and slick-back hair. All were on the house committee and relentless advocates for change.

"Look at them," said Martin. "The three stooges."

"The three witches," said Hector.

"Not the Scottish play! I beg you!" Roly Poly held his hands up as if to ward-off an unseen evil presence.

"The three silks, then," said Hector. "Smooth silk, man-made silk . . . and . . ."

"Silk and rayon mix," offered Martin.

"Their position on women members is blatant virtue-signalling," said Purdey. "They don't want to spoil their prospects in front of a Judicial Appointments Board."

Martin suggested that, from what he had heard, the chance of their ever sitting as judges of the High Court was fanciful to the point of delusional, so there must be other reasons.

"Do they realise where all this is heading?" said Purdey. "The women will elect each other."

"They will breed," said Martin.

"In no time, there'll be women on the committees."

"They'll be running them," said Hector.

"Women members can bring women guests," said Purdey ominously.

"Imagine—a table of four of them in the coffee room!"

"The noise!"

"And to think they call us misogynist!" said Martin.

Their loud laughter clearly irritated the 'pro women' group of lawyers, journos and thesps the other end of the bar, who ostentatiously moved further away.

"Look here," said 'Roly Poly' Rowlands, star of stage and screen. "I couldn't be more on-side, but I can't be seen hanging out with you *status quo* boys or I'll never work again. Keep up the good fight."

"Oh, don't go," said Martin, with no attempt at sincerity.

Roly Poly gave an apologetic smile and shuffled off to join the theatre director, with whom he promptly agreed, *sotto voce,* that the club's stance against women membership was an embarrassing anachronism in the 21st century.

"I don't think the fact Roly Poly is out of work has anything to do with being seen with us," said Martin. "She's a terrible old ham. I saw her playing Pastor Manders at the Gielgud a few years ago—it was like watching the school play. Unbearable. I don't think she's worked since."

A tall figure appeared in the archway leading from the bar to the main staircase and marched towards them, heavily, like the Commendatore in Don Giovani.

"Christ!" said Hector. "Sorry, vicar. But the Brigadier looks like he's seen his own ghost!"

The Brigadier was actually a General. Specifically, Lieutenant General Sir Simeon Wallace-Black, KBE, CB. He strode into the room without his usual swagger, his face drawn and livid. A club servant had his double malt poured before he had asked for it. He downed it in one and turned to Purdey.

"Sprats has fallen!" he said, as though Sprats were France in 1940.

"Sprats? You're kidding!"

"Women members. With immediate effect."

"Sprats? Has he gone mad? What do the men have to say?"

"Doesn't matter a damn what they say. He owns the place. He can do what he likes."

There was an awful silence.

The little cabal of 'pro-women' reformers had obviously heard the news. Smooth silk raised his glass to the general and with a ghastly smile called over:

"It's only a matter of time!"

Patrick Rowlands kept his back firmly towards his erstwhile friends.

"Why can't they leave us alone?" said Hector, somewhat pathetically. "All I want to do is spend the occasional evening with some chums."

"It's hardly your fault that you have no female chums," said Purdey.

"Fuck off!"

"If you wanted to tour around South London on a carnival float," said Martin, "dressed in latex, wearing a woman's wig and false tits, they would cheer you from the pavements."

"They would celebrate your diversity," said Purdey.

"Sprats," said the general, shaking his head. "Sprats!"

"*'That it should come to this'*," said Hector.

"*'But two months dead'*," said Martin.

2 Problem solved

Ambrose Harding rather enjoyed the nickname given him by the younger members—"Ambrose Hard of Hearing"—and he often played up to it.

"I'm sorry dear boy, what was that?"

"I was merely suggesting, chairman, that since it is only a newspaper report, we should hold our nerve and do nothing."

The scene was the monthly meeting of the house committee, over which Ambrose Harding presided as chairman. The 'dear boy' was a Court of Appeal judge. The newspaper report concerned the publication of the complete list of Macready's members.

"This sort of thing is very damaging," said the judge irritably.

He was a tall, imposing figure: 6 feet two in height, and with his long nose and cruel eyes it was sometimes said he looked like a gannet. On and off the bench, he was in a near-constant state of irritation. It was his misfortune to be a distant relative of the 50s actor James Robertson Justice, and to bear his surname. 'Lord Justice Justice' was a source of merriment at the junior Bar, and to his distaste he had figured in a Times Diary series about nominative determinism. It irked him, more than he let it show, that if ever he were promoted to the Supreme Court he would become 'Lord Justice'—which would *sound* as though he were still in the Court of Appeal. His brother judges and senior members of Macready's called him "JJ". As far as he was concerned, the publication of his name as a member of Macready's was a personal humiliation, and the sooner the club allowed women in, the better.

"No doubt the other papers will run with it," said Pierre Moreau, the Club Secretary of more than five years, who had recently been given honorary membership and liked to exercise the privilege of contributing to these meetings.

Pierre knew everything there was to know about the clubs of Europe and North America. He had been member and secretary of some of them and gave the impression of having been member and secretary of all of them. Although as secretary he should perhaps have been impartial in such matters, or at least given the impression of impartiality, he made no secret of the fact that he was an ardent enthusiast for a mixed membership of Macready's.

"We're becoming a laughing-stock," said JJ.

"But any response is bound to make things worse, don't you think?" said the smooth silk we have already met, and to whom respect (if not deference) requires he should be given a name: Quentin Latimer KC. One of the highest-earning silks in the Temple.

"I think, if we have patience, the current hysteria will burn itself out naturally," said Docter Hans Fleischer. Hans was a consultant psychiatrist at St. Mary Bethlehem, and familiarly known in the club as 'Sigmund'. He saw everything in terms of a mental health issue susceptible to treatment. He was resolutely against Macready's opening its doors to women members. It would 'upset the dynamic', he said. He wasn't wholly persuaded they should be allowed to practice psychiatry.

"I agree," said silk & rayon mix, the criminal defence barrister in the shiny suit, who rarely had anything original to offer.

"To engage with the issue will only increase the women's sense of victimhood," said Hans Fleischer. "Which they crave, Ya? It is the classic narcissistic grandiosity."

"Absolutely," said silk and rayon.

"Maybe so," said Ambrose, wondering what the hell 'Sigmund' Fleischer was talking about. "But, if Hans will forgive me, we have a more pressing issue to contend with."

"More pressing than this?" barked man-made silk, waving a newspaper as though to the benches on the other side of the House of Commons.

The paper had his name (Saul Trencherman MP) and his photograph (unflatteringly over-weight) prominently set within a report to the effect that misogynist lawyers and politicians '*conspire to keep women out of the exclusive boys-own Macready's Club*'.

"You will no doubt form you own view, when you hear what Ambrose has to tell us," said JJ.

"I will form mine, even if Saul doesn't form his," said Quentin.

Ambrose sighed and continued—

"This afternoon I received a draft resolution which, as I understand our rules, I am obliged to put before the upcoming EGM."

"It was handed to me this morning," said Pierre. He wanted it to be clear who, in fact, had actually received it.

"And passed to me," said Ambrose, wearily, "this afternoon. It is from Hector Floodgate."

"Oh, him!" said JJ.

"I rather like him," said Hans.

"Really?" said Pierre.

"Shall I read it, or not?"

Hans peered at Ambrose over his bifocals, and noting his irritation said, in his consulting room voice—

"Of course, my dear chairman."

"Please do," said silk & rayon, not to be left out of things.

Ambrose cleared his throat and gave the house committee a painfully matter-of-fact delivery of -

RESOLUTION

Macready's Club celebrates Diversity, Equality and Inclusivity and RESOLVES that the following amendment be made to the Club's Rules:

That Rule 3 be amended by substitution of the following words—

(a) Membership of the Club shall henceforth be open to women.

"About bloody time!" said JJ.

"Maybe the young fool has a brain after all," said Saul Trencherman.

"I rather suspect there's more," said Quentin, uber-calm and with a cold smile. "You said (a), chairman. Is there a (b)?"

Ambrose cleared his throat again, and continued -

(b) No candidate without a penis shall be eligible for membership.

*

Hector's closest friends smiled at his joke but urged him to withdraw the motion ASAP. He refused. His enemies turned their backs on him in the bar. "Not funny" evolved into "Appalling bad taste."

Martin told him he was enjoying the controversy too much. The general told him he was damaging 'the cause'. Dr. Fleischer bought him a drink and suggested it might be the better course to steer clear of controversy.

But Hector stubbornly held his ground, relishing the upset he had created, far more than even Martin had challenged him.

When Lord Justice Justice bearded Hector in the coffee room one night and asked him '*what the hell did he think he was playing at* ', Hector—who was not at all drunk—told the Court of Appeal judge, to '*go fuck himself, in every conceivable way*'.

3 The Broom Cupboard

There was a little room on the ground floor of Macready's, to the left of the main staircase. And because there was no door, it was open to the view of anyone entering the club—members and guests alike—unless a thick velvet curtain were drawn across its opening. The space had become known, with fond self-deprecation, as "the broom cupboard". And in that broom cupboard had sat Lord Chief Justices, Prime Ministers, Governors of the Bank of England, Ambassadors, editors of national newspapers, giants of industry and commerce—engaged (so the Bugle would have it) in discussing affairs of state in which no woman's voice had been heard these last one hundred and fifty years.

It was in the broom cupboard, curtain drawn, that James Purdey, Martin (he of the dog-collar), Roly Poly, the general, 'Sigmund' Fleischer and JJ were taking their various positions in a heated discussion after a good lunch, one Friday afternoon. Hector's draft proposal was the subject.

"It's a very foolish stunt," said the general. "It may be funny, but if he thinks it will do the cause any good, he needs his head examined."

"The cause?" said JJ.

Dr. Fleischer, looked studiously at JJ, as he would at a patient, the tips of his fingers lightly touching each other. But he quickly looked away when the judge caught his eye.

"It's brilliant," said Martin.

"Why 'brilliant'?" asked Roly Poly, eager to understand.

"Because it doesn't discriminate against women."

"Of course it discriminates against women," snapped JJ.

"With respect, judge, it doesn't. It only discriminates against people who do not have a penis," said Purdey. "The absence of a penis is not a protected characteristic under the Equality Act."

"The whole thing is absurd," said the judge.

"I don't dissent from that," said Purdey.

"Oh, don't you?" said JJ, bristling. "Then who knows? I may be right after all."

Dr. Fleischer was now more interested in the increasing tension between JJ and Purdey, but he remained detached from the scene as though observing it in his consulting rooms through a one-way mirror.

James Purdey the fighter soldiered on—

"But in strict law, according to the suggested amendment, surely anyone, including a woman, can join Macready's, so long as they have a penis. And a penis—"

"Is not a protected characteristic. I do get the point," said JJ. "But it wouldn't stand up in my court."

"An unfortunate way of putting it, in the circumstances," said Martin.

"The amendment is frivolous, vexatious, offensive and REPUGNANT! And in my opinion—*my judgment*—if any such rule were challenged it would be struck out as unlawful."

The general was hardly able to get his words out between bursts of laughter.

"With the greatest respect, old boy..."

He shook his head, sneezed, took forever blowing his nose on a huge, red handkerchief and said—

"I've yet to meet one of you lot," he pointed at the stony-faced judge, "brave enough, in the current climate, to rule that *as a matter of law* a woman cannot have a penis."

With that he left the broom cupboard. His laughter could be heard all the way down the passageway to the cloakroom.

An awkward silence was broken by Saul Trencherman MP— "*I'd better be off to the House*". Martin looked at his watch, said "*Dear Lord! Is that the time?*" and drifted away. Purdey said "*Damn! My clerks are texting me*". And one by one the others made their excuses and departed— "*My train leaves Liverpool Street at 4:30*"— "*I should probably change for the Opera*"— "*I have a patient. I mustn't keep her waiting. Ya?*"— until the old judge was left alone, sitting in a cracked-leather armchair, staring moodily into the middle-distance and swilling the remains of his brandy round and round in a heavy glass tumbler.

Suddenly, but not at all violently, he rose to his feet as though he had at last made up his mind on a thought that had been troubling him. He finished his brandy in one swig and made to leave, but at that very moment the broom cupboard curtain was thrown to one side and Quentin Latimer stood in the entrance, slightly drunk and clinging to the velvet like an actor taking a curtain-call.

"Have you seen this?".

He tottered towards JJ and thrust a copy of the Evening Bugle at his hands.

"A hundred or so lawyers—*none of them members might I add*—have signed a petition—*a petition! would you believe the cheek?*—demanding that we change our rules."

The judge snatched the newspaper from him and read aloud:

"Top lawyers urge London's Macready's Club to overturn sexist membership policy"

"Top lawyers indeed!" he muttered, and continued:

"Membership of Macready's Club provides practising lawyers, young and old, with invaluable networking opportunities among high-ranking members of the judiciary, which are of significant advantage to them professionally. Women, however, are expressly barred from joining Macready's, effectively denying them those career opportunities. This discriminatory practice is a contributory factor to the significant and deeply regrettable underrepresentation of women in top-tier positions within legal profession and the judiciary."

"I have never understood," he said, "the obsession in the media with the so-called advantage young barristers are said to have by joining Macready's and 'forming connections' with the judiciary. That wretched woman in the Bugle writes of little else."

"She's a character in Dickens, isn't she?" said Quentin, laughing at his own joke and hiccupping as he did so. "Little Else," he explained.

The judge ignored him.

"If ever the conceited young puppy who goes by the name of James Purdey KC should have the misfortune to appear in my court," he folded up the Evening Bugle and smiled as close to benignly as was possible for him, "I would endeavour, with every faculty I possess, to find reasons to rule against him."

"Surely not," oozed the smooth silk.

"And his client."

The judged eyed Quentin steadily, not at all pleasantly, and asked "Who do you think is leaking the club's affairs to the press?"

Perhaps because he was the worse for red wine, or maybe he had other reasons for being ill at ease, Quentin was unable to maintain the sphinx-like composure for which he was renowned when batting an awkward question from the Supreme Court bench.

"I . . . I really have no idea," he said.

"Would you tell me, if you did?"

Quentin did not reply, but a mischievous imp surfing the alcohol coursing through his bloodstream whispered to his brain "Tell the old gannet you think it's him."

"Whoever it is,' said the judge, leaning forward as though about to dive at a mackerel.

"Whoever it is . . . " faltered Quentin.

"Deserves a medal," said the judge, to Quentin's utter astonishment.

"A medal?"

Quentin took the opportunity to sit down.

"Macready's will never admit women unless it is *shamed* into doing so."

JJ snarled the word '*shamed*'.

"And it will never be *shamed* until its affairs are an open book and the whole of London is either laughing at us or condemning us. The party line may well be that these relentless press reports are damaging the club—but I wouldn't be so sure. If anything, they're not damaging it enough."

He paused for a reaction—but there was none.

"Let me put to you an alternative analysis: that the public demand for reform is growing so great, and our kudos is diminishing to so little, as to leave the traditional *status quo* numb-skull members of this once-great club no option but to abandon their misogynistic stance or belong to a club that is the pariah of London. And which do *you* think the members will choose when push comes to shove? When they are faced with a vote at the EGM? Eh? When the Macready tie, which they so love to wear on television, is no longer a badge of honour, but a mark of *shame*. Do you think they will keep up the good fight *on principle*? Of course not. Self-interest will triumph over principle. It always does. Roll on the EGM, and let's get this farce done and dusted once and for all. Bravo to the whistle-blower, I say. Give him a medal."

Quentin remained silent, the obsequious smile on his face tending towards the simpering.

"This draft resolution of Hector Floodgate's for example," continued the judge. "It will never be put to the members of course. Hector confided to me, privately, that he only did it to make a point—God knows what!—and that he would withdraw it before the meeting."

(JJ had an ability to lie without the least tell-tale signs.)

"I have no doubt he meant what he said."

(Was JJ thinking of his encounter with Hector in the coffee room?)

"So. Our members, whichever side they are on, will not have the pleasure of voting on Hector's ridiculous proposal after all."

At last Quentin found himself able to speak. "That's a relief... Isn't it?"

"No. it's a pity," said JJ. "A great pity. The Bugle has a proxy reporter at every closed meeting we hold."

Quentin sank a little lower in his chair.

"What would the general public have thought, informed by the Today Programme, Sky News, Channel 4, the whole pack of them, what would they have made of Hector

Floodgate's obscene little stunt if it had been widely known, I wonder?"

JJ leaned forward confidentially.

"Suppose '*the penis proposal*' had remained on the agenda. Suppose a Bugle reporter had infiltrated the meeting or peered over the shoulder of a member on his computer. Suppose they heard the motion put to the vote. That would have been a story and a half, wouldn't it? Better still, suppose someone *leaked* it before the meeting even took place? What would the public make of *that*? Eh? Now there's a question!"

He smiled mirthlessly at Quentin.

"I suppose we will never know the answer."

The judge busily pulled open the Evening Bugle and began reading it as though Quentin were not in the room.

*

It was too late to catch the Saturday papers, but the Sunday Reflector printed Hector's proposal in full, under the headline -

Macready's only accepts members with members

The Bugle carried a coruscating editorial written by Isadora Jarre, citing what she called the 'lad's culture' of the club, and pouring scorn on an 'adolescent *status quo* group' she had identified, mentioning some of its members by name, focusing on the Hon. Hector Floodgate—'*the privileged son of an aristocrat whose wealth derives from slave trading*'.

A three-pronged assault followed. Other newspapers were unanimous in demanding '*Elite, boys-only clubs like Macready's should open their doors, and their minds, to women members.*'

Baroness Cleethorpes (a very Cross Bencher, past President of the Commission for Inclusion) publicly castigated any male judge who remained a member.

And in the House of Commons, an Early Day Motion urged Macready's to '*reflect on its commitment to equality and diversity and immediately abolish its outrageous centuries-old ban on women members*'.

An opinion piece in the Bugle was given front-page prominence. It read —

> **Recent exposés have brought to light a deeply troubling 'laddish' culture in Macready's, an exclusive London gentlemen's club.**
>
> **Each to his immature own, you might say. But of real concern is that many prominent public figures, including judges, Members of Parliament, bishops and university chancellors are members of Macready's.**
>
> **Their continued affiliation can only signal a tacit approval of the misogynist, public school fun-and-games that this newspaper has reported over the past months; not the least repugnant of which is this latest in a long history, a disgusting resolution proposed by Hon. Hector Floodgate (photograph above), apparently for serious consideration at the club's imminent extraordinary general meeting.**
>
> **It is unacceptable for anyone in whom the public places its trust—whether they be entrusted with upholding justice, representing constituents, providing moral leadership or overseeing higher education—to belong to an institution that at**

best turns a blind eye, and at worst secretly enjoys, misogynist tropes such as those this newspaper has repeatedly condemned.

Macready's membership overwhelmingly comprises privileged white men, making it profoundly unrepresentative of the diverse society which public figures are meant to serve. The resignation from Macready's of all judges, Members of Parliament, bishops and university chancellors, is long overdue. It is high time they left the sixth-form common room behind them, stepped into the real world, and behaved like responsible adults.

The author was a certain Brigit van der Linden, barrister at law.

4 Brigit

Brigit van der Linden was proud of her Dutch name, not because she had any affinity with the Netherlands or its people, but because it signalled that she was from immigrant stock. "*My great grandparents were immigrants*" she would say, meaning that her opinions about the United Kingdom's international obligations to asylum-seekers trumped anybody else's opinions—"*so let's leave it at that, shall we?*"

She was a prominent 'human rights' barrister: a self-employed, self-publicised, self-obsessed, sole practitioner. Working mainly from a small flat in Red Lion Street, Holborn, she had an arrangement with nearby chambers in Gray's Inn, who for an agreed monthly payment provided her with limited administrative services—occasional use of a meeting room, use of printer/copier, and some basic clerking.

Brigit's guiding lights, her triplet goddesses, were 'diversity', 'equality' and 'inclusivity'. In Brigit's inclusive world there was no room for anyone who did not share her passion for diversity and equality—especially of the sexes.

While some barristers have a 'commercial' practice, and others have a 'criminal' practice or a 'chancery' practice, Brigit van der Linden had what might be called a 'grievance' practice. She only looked after the hard-done-by, or those who thought they were hard-done-by, or could be persuaded they were hard-done-by. Highly visible on social media, she trawled Twitter and Facebook for people with grievances, whom she rooted-out with the enthusiasm of a pig rooting-out truffles—and she was of inestimable help in identifying for them grievances they never thought they had, or even knew existed as species of grievance. Fearless of the Bar Council, she touted for work on the Internet, as untouchable as an Uber driver unlawfully plying for hire on the streets of London. Her profile was *@andtheytrytoshutmeup*, her banner picture was the Statue of Liberty, and her 'pinned tweet' was the clarion text—

> **Give me your tired, your poor, Your huddled masses yearning to breathe free, The wretched of your teeming shore. Send these, the homeless, tempest-tossed to me, I lift my lamp beside the golden door.**

She had several thousand 'followers'.

Although senior in call and well up to the demands of it, Brigit had not applied for silk on principle: she deplored the selection process as sexist, racist, classist and any other "ist" knocking around.

It would be inappropriate to offer any physical description of Brigit van der Linden—whether she was handsome or homely, whether svelt or muscular, tall or short—because to do so would *objectify* her; and if I even tip-toed in that direction, her very name might leap from the page to berate me. Suffice it that she had lank, thinning grey hair, the victim of a poorly executed blue rinse, that looked as though it had never been washed since the rinsing of it; she wore thick-rimmed glasses; and every man in her proxy Gray's Inn chambers was terrified of her.

Macready's was anathema to Brigit van der Linden. It would be an exaggeration to say that it epitomised *everything* that she despised (no institution could possibly be that inclusive), but it ticked a good number of the boxes. It reeked of male chauvinism. It was a revolting boys-only networking hub, a stepping-stone on a path to preferment denied to women. She loathed the place. She loathed its members.

She loathed "*the vulgar Macready tie*". She loathed "*the smug air of entitlement*" that "*polluted*" the atmosphere. Although an indefatigable campaigner for the reform of Macready's, Brigit vowed she would never allow herself to be put up for membership when the campaign was won—which, she said, was inevitable. She even refused, point blank, "*to cross its vile threshold*" when she was invited by a reforming member as his guest—and she posted her refusal on Twitter and Facebook, so that the world should see her displeasure. "*Wild horses couldn't drag me into Macready's,*" she wrote. To be frank, it is unlikely that wild horses would stand much of a chance in *any* encounter with Brigit van der Linden.

Articulate and outspoken, Brigit occasionally appeared on the BBC's 'Question Time' and was a favourite of its famously balanced audience. Not long after the club's membership list had been leaked to the press and the next day's headlines had crowed about its being "*a glossary of the British establishment*", Saul Trencherman MP found himself on the Question Time panel in the role of OQTP—'Official Question Time Punchbag'. Having survived a few sharp jabs about the cost-of-living crisis, he was still recoiling from a savage left hook concerning Bibby Stockholm and the upgrading of its Sky TV subscription to include the full sports package and premium movies, when Brigit van der Linden moved in and thwacked him hard below the belt.

"Do you give tuppence for Diversity, Equality and Inclusivity?" she said, the sheer force of her delivery flinging her backwards in her chair.

"Of course I do!"

(Derisive hoots from the audience.)

"Then why don't you do the decent thing and resign from Macready's Club?"

The audience erupted with applause. Trencherman's co-panellists guffawed—there was only one side it was prudent to be on, and it wasn't Macready's.

The show's host cut in over the ruckus—

"I think the question was about immigration—not discrimination".

(More laughter, whistles, and applause.)

"Shall we take another? Brenda, are you there?" A middle-aged woman raised her hand. "What's your question?"

Brenda began to speak before a microphone had been dangled above her, and she had to start again when it was. She read her question from a crumpled piece of paper—

"If he loses his seat at the general election, would Saul consider going on 'I'm a celebrity, get me out of here?'"

Before he could answer, Brigit called out—"Only if women aren't allowed in the Jungle!"

*

Lord Justice Justice turned off the television in his cold Lincoln's Inn flat, even while it was still rolling the credits for that Thursday's edition of 'Question Time'. He lifted the telephone and dialled a number, slowly and carefully on an old-fashioned rotary dial, and waited for a reply. It took so long to come, he was on the point of ending the call when . . .

"Yes?"

"Did you watch it?"

"I did."

"And?"

"It's now or never, isn't it? '*There is a tide*' and all that."

"Then do it."

*

On returning to her flat in Red Lion Street, Brigit picked up a Delphic message on her answer machine: a familiar voice simply told her to "check email". Intrigued, she promptly checked, and sure enough, buried amongst her daily hate-mail was a message flagged "important". The subject was "Macready's", and the sender was her trusted whistle-blower, who went by the name (rather unflattering of Brigit) '**SourceForTheGoose**'. The message was simple—

> **Please find the attached legal Opinion of Quentin Latimer KC**

Brigit downloaded it and read it. Three times. Then she started typing. It was one-thirty in the morning before she was satisfied with her Press Release.

*

London had not yet woken-up, but the front page of the Bugle Online already carried what it called a 'news flash'—

> **Leading KC says Macready's ban on women membership is unlawful**

Beneath the headline was an opinion piece by Brigit van der Linden:

> **The disgraceful ban on women membership of Macready's has finally been exposed as unlawful. This outrageous wrong to women, perpetuated over many decades—contrary to the common law of the land, not to mention common decency—is crying out to be righted.**

If Macready's is to have any hope of salvaging even a sliver of credibility from the remains of its reputation, its unlawful practices need to be revisited with the greatest possible expedition,

We look forward to learning that proposals of women as candidates for membership of Macready's are given immediate precedence over the weary list of male supplicants currently waiting to be elected. Only when there is an even split of men and women members will the sins of Macready's past be absolved.

5 A matter of opinion

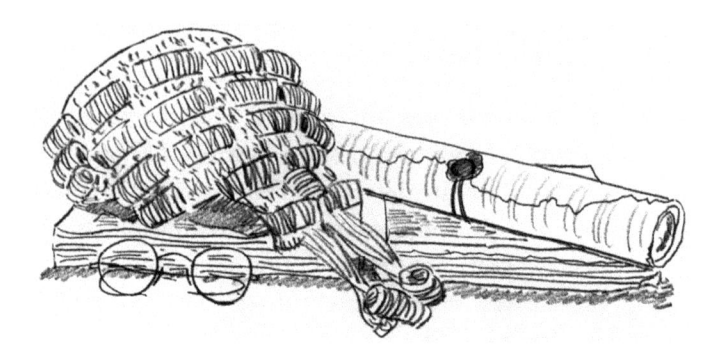

"Can someone explain to me, in words of one syllable, what Quentin has actually said?"

They had gathered in the pretty gardens of the Wayfarers Club, far from the eyes and ears of the enemy at Macready's.

"That won't be easy, general," said Purdey. "Quentin's opinions tend to be written in words of three syllables or more."

"In plain English then, and bugger the syllable count."

"Quentin has presented the club with written advice—"

"Which the club did not ask for," interrupted Hector.

"He has *volunteered* an 'Opinion', signed by him and co-signed by a junior in his chambers—"

"The junior probably wrote it," said Martin.

"That would explain things," said Hector.

"The junior is window dressing," said Purdey, "to make it look more authoritative."

"Get on with it!" said the general. "What *is* the great Quentin Latimer KC's bloody opinion which nobody asked for?"

"That in ordinary English usage 'a woman' can be 'a gentleman'."

"WHAT?"

"That in ordinary English usage 'a woman' can be 'a gentleman'."

"That's bollocks!" said the general.

"It would seem they're irrelevant," said Martin.

"What's the legal term?" asked Hector.

"*Testiculis est.*"

"Can you boys *please* speak English?"

"Of course his opinion is bollocks," said Purdey, "and Quentin Latimer knows it as well as anyone."

"Then why did he say it?"

"Quentin sees himself as Socrates," said Martin. "Spinning a 'noble lie' for the greater good of an inferior membership who don't know what's best for them."

"A '*noble* lie'? They *rank* them these days?"

"If we can be persuaded to live with the absurd fiction that when the club's rules say 'gentlemen' they really mean 'ladies and gentlemen'," said Purdey, "then Macready's can elect women members right away."

"No need to change the rules," said Martin.

"More importantly, no need for a *two-thirds majority* in favour of changing them," said Purdey.

"Which is the point of the whole shabby exercise," said Hector. "A rule change by the back door."

"A rule change in breach of our rules," said Purdey.

"Perhaps I was too kind likening him to Socrates," said Martin. "Quentin is more of a Humpty Dumpty. A rule means whatever he wants it to mean."

"I think he's more of a Mad Hatter," said the general. "If the rules mean whatever we want them to mean, what's the point of having them?"

Hector said he knew a great many members, good friends and stalwarts of the club, who might reluctantly cross their fingers and go along with Quentin's nonsense '*just to get the Bugle off their backs*'.

"Shortsighted," said the general. "What'll be the next rule that Quentin and the house committee decide means whatever they want it to mean?"

No one volunteered a guess. Their sombre reflections were broken by Hector -

"Talking of the house committee, I have been summoned by the headmaster and the prefects to appear before them next Thursday."

"What?"

"Why?"

"They want me to apologise to JJ."

"Apologise for what?"

"I told him to go fuck himself."

"And did he?" asked Martin.

"We were in the coffee room."

"Were there many people there?"

"Packed. All the side tables full."

"Why on earth did you tell him to fuck off?"

"I didn't. I told him to go fuck himself in every conceivable way."

"Hector!"

"He shouted at me. So I shouted back."

"'It was a tad strong old bean," said Purdey. "Were you drunk?"

"As sober as he was."

"Are you *going* to apologise?" asked the general.

"Fuck no! Why should I? He started it."

"What do you think they will do to you?"

"I don't care."

"No good will come of this," said Martin.

"*Ex turpi causa* . . . ," said Purdey.

"Oh for Christ's sake!" said the general.

6 Protest

Brigit van Der Linden was determined that a protest should take place '*while the iron was hot*' and as soon as practicable after the sensational leaking of Quentin Latimer's opinion. She also wanted the timing of it to have a certain poignancy, so she decided on the evening of the next meeting of Macready's house committee—the date of which 'SourceForTheGoose' was happy to give her.

No stranger to organising demonstrations, and a contributor to 'The Activists Handbook', Brigit was acutely aware that a flash protest required all the pre-publicity she could muster. She plastered social media with an automated, half-hourly recurring, call-to-arms; addressed to "*all women who care about gender equality*", urging them to attend an important demonstration outside Macready's Club in protest against its "*systematic exclusions of women, other than as cleaners or waiters or guests of privileged white men*".

She made a large banner for herself, adapted from an earlier protest:

> **What do we want? EQUALITY!**
>
> **When do we want it? 150 years ago!**

She suggested texts for *ad hoc*, bannerless protestors, who might have been uncertain of the target—

> **Macready's—open your doors to EQUALITY!**
>
> **Let women IN !**
>
> **WOMEN ARE JUDGES TOO !**

She was very pleased with her clever play on words—

Say NO to Boy's Club (IN) JUSTICE

—and was disappointed no one understood it.

And perhaps she should have thought twice about the curious—

There's no 'I' in Macready's

In case attendance were thin—which, at such short notice, was her principal concern—Brigit called-in some favours from protestor colleagues in 'Extinction Rebellion', 'Just Stop Oil', 'Black Lives Matter', and the Junior Doctors; who happily agreed to come along and boost the numbers, whatever the cause, there being no other public protest scheduled for that day.

Finally, she drafted a petition, which she intended to hand to the chairman personally, or if not to him, to any hapless member she could lay her hands on. It was in quintessential, full-blown Brigit-speak.

> The sexist attitudes promoted by clubs like Macready's have real-world consequences, contributing to barriers faced by women and marginalised groups in politics, the justice system, religious institutions and academia. Continued membership of such an organisation by those in positions of authority implies and validates that elitist "old boys' networks" still hold sway while progress towards genuine equality remains elusive.
>
> It is no longer defensible in the 21st century for public figures to affiliate themselves with a club that discriminates based on gender and socioeconomic status. As such, we demand that all judges,

MPs, bishops and university chancellors who are currently members of Macready's immediately resign their memberships.

Only by disavowing Macready's and similar institutions can these leaders demonstrate a true commitment to the principles of equality, inclusivity and meritocracy we expect in a modern multicultural Britain. Their resignations would send a powerful message that the days of tolerating entrenched sexism and elitism from those in positions of influence are over.

When at last the big day came, Brigit alerted her trusted 'on-side' newspapers and TV stations and set off early from her flat in Holborn, with an A4 brown manilla envelope in her hand, on which was written in bold font:

To the Chairman, Macready's Club: PETITION

*

Ambrose Harding called the meeting to order and said that the first item on the Agenda was, of course, the Hector Floodgate affair.

"We have your statement, JJ. Has Hector put in *anything* in response, Pierre?"

"Nothing," said the secretary.

"Then would you show him in, please?"

Pierre left the committee room and returned with Hector nonchalantly walking a few paces behind him.

"Would you like to take a seat?" asked Ambrose.

"No. Thank you. I'd prefer to stand," replied Hector. "This isn't going to take long, is it?"

"Stand then. You know why we asked you to come here tonight?"

"Actually, I don't. For the life of me, I can't think of any reason whatsoever. Unless it's my draft resolution? That ruffled a few feathers, didn't it just!"

Hector smiled disarmingly at JJ.

"You received my letter, and Lord Justice Justice's statement?"

"Oh that. What about it?"

"Are you going to apologise?"

"Which one of us are you asking? JJ or me?"

"You know perfectly well."

"What I know perfectly well is that JJ most certainly owes *me* an apology."

The judge stared at him, his otherwise implacable face showing the faintest beginnings of an unpleasant sneer—familiar to the Bar when he sat listening to the ramblings of a prisoner giving the evidence that would see him spending the rest of his life in jail.

"You do understand, Hector," said Ambrose kindly, "that we are considering suspension?"

"Oh, I wouldn't dream of asking you to *suspend* JJ."

"This is getting nowhere," said Saul Trencherman. "Are you going to apologise or not?"

"Of course not," said Hector, looking directly at the judge. And summoning as much insolence as he could cram into just three words, he asked "Is that all?"

Not receiving a reply, he looked around the room carelessly and left. Though his manner had been easy enough in front of the house committee, his hand trembled as he took a drink in the bar.

The vote was unanimous. Hector had squandered any hope of suspension. It was expulsion. For 'conduct unbecoming a gentleman'.

"Five minutes break?" suggested JJ casually.

*

Ambrose again called the meeting to order and asked that the minutes show that he had requested Quentin Latimer KC to leave the room while his Opinion was discussed.

"For the record, Pierre," said Lord Justice Justice, "the correct wording is that Quentin has '*recused*' himself."

"Quite so."

"Thank you, Quentin," said Ambrose. "If you would?"

Smooth silk rose from his seat, and with a pretence of modesty that made a poor disguise of unassailable self-confidence he said, "*Don't be too hard on me.*"

"No, no. By no means," said Ambrose. "We are indebted to you Quentin. It's ... it's an excellent piece of work. Invaluable. Thank you so much."

"An elegant solution to an otherwise intractable problem," said JJ.

"Absolutely," said Saul Trencherman.

"Many thanks," chipped in silk and rayon mix—who, it is quite possible, had not read it.

Quentin opened the door, and making sure to look at each member of the house committee in turn, he left the room. And after a short pause, no one knowing who should speak first, the general said—

"I've never read such bollocks in my life."

"It may well be 'bollocks', as you so eloquently put it," said the judge. "But you are missing the point."

"Which is?"

"That it serves the greater good."

"Dear God! Not that again!"

The general left the table to pour himself a drink.

"On the back of a lie," said Dr. Fleischer.

"A noble lie."

(A loud splash of soda from the general's direction.)

"But a lie nonetheless."

"It's blindingly obvious, for God's sake," said the general, coming back to the table with a large whiskey. "An intelligent child could tell you. The Club's rules do NOT permit women to be members. Simple as that. They NEVER HAVE. And there is absolutely NOTHING unlawful about it."

"It's been our position for decades," said Dr. Fleischer, calmly.

"And it's been affirmed at AGM after AGM after EGM after EGM after Special Bloody General Meeting after . . . "

The general's blood pressure was heading off the scale . . .

" . . . that if women are to become members of Macready's, THE RULES HAVE TO BLOODY WELL CHANGE."

"Which requires a two-thirds majority vote of members," said JJ, patiently.

"Which we know from experience," added Saul Trencherman, "is never going to happen."

"So we just *claim* that a club rule means whatever we want it to mean, do we?" said the general. "Like Humpty Dumpty?"

"Humpty Dumpty? What the devil are you talking about?" said JJ.

"Humpty Dumpty. 'Alice in Wonderland' — "

Loud shouts of "**Shame on you!**" from the street below interrupted his answer.

"Now what?"

The door burst open, and Quentin rushed back into the room. "Have you seen what's going on outside?"

The general went to a sash window, pulled it open and leaned right out.

"Mind you don't fall!" said Ambrose.

"Or we'll never be able to put you together again," said Quentin, recklessly giving away that he had been listening at the door. "And it's '*Through the Looking Glass*', not '*Alice in Wonderland*'."

"There must be hundreds of them," said the general, his head still out of the window. "There's a couple of your lot," he pulled his head back in and nodded to JJ, "in wigs."

"Judges?"

"Don't be daft. Barristers. Wimmin in wigs."

"Let me see."

JJ stuck his head out of the window.

Derisive hoots and cries of "**Women are judges too!**" greeted his appearance. Someone threw an empty paper cup towards him. Although it fell short by two or three metres, JJ was startled and retreated a little.

"**Shame on you!**" shouted one of the young female barristers parading the street in her wig and gown, looking straight at the judge.

"This is simply appalling," said JJ. "Bar Council territory."

"My turn, move over." Saul Trencherman nudged JJ out of the way.

"Christ! They have Channel Four there." The MP was back into the room fast as greased lightning.

Next it was silk and rayon, the Old Bailey hack, who peeked out of the window.

"That's odd! I thought he was still inside. It's one of mine."

An almighty roar erupted from the crowd as a chauffeur-driven Mercedes drew up at the kerbside. Ambrose went to the window and took a cautious look. A middle-aged man wearing the Macready tie left the vehicle as quickly as he could and tried to force his way through the baying crowd, who shouted—

"Privileged White Man!"

At one point he was completely surrounded and might never have made it into the club, had he not been rescued by the hall porter, a menacing-looking Scot, on whose appearance the crowd parted, enough to let the distressed member through.

Ambrose grabbed a telephone and punched the speed-dial button for the hall porter, who answered almost immediately.

"Lock the front gates," he said.

Then it began to rain. First a light drizzle, but in no time a tropical downpour.

If anyone hoped the rain might break the protest up, they were to be sorely disappointed. The sudden deluge made the crowd as angry as wasps. The 'extinction rebellion' swarm flew around, madly trying to find a dry surface on which to glue themselves. The 'just stop oil' swarm hovered in their bewilderment, buzzing with frustration that the paint they sprayed on the club's old walls was washed away before any legible words could be written.

The core protesters, the stout *'women for equality'*, were, if the truth be told, all for returning to their dry homes, but reluctantly felt they had to stay if their supporters did. Their fury against all mankind, particularly the hall porter who had locked the club doors against them and made them protest in the rain, boiled their blood to the very edge of hyperpyrexia.

Brigit, delivering it as though she were Queen Elizabeth I at Tilbury, or Flora Robson in the film, declaimed the words of her petition, which she knew by heart, through a megaphone—

> **"The sexist attitudes promoted by clubs like Macready's have real-world consequences... "**

In her own way, she looked quite magnificent. Standing defiantly against the storm, her bedraggled clothes dripping with water, the brown manilla envelope soggy and limp in her left hand, the megaphone in her right, her face contorted with anger.

> **"It is no longer defensible in the 21st century for public figures to affiliate themselves with a club that discriminates based on gender... "**

The other side of Macready's great wooden doors, Hector Floodgate was arguing with the hall porter.

"The chairman has ordered me to keep the doors locked, SIR."

Somehow, the Scotsman managed to make "SIR" sound like an insult.

"I am aware of that. But I want to leave."

Brigit droned on through her megaphone—

> **"It is unacceptable for anyone in whom the public places its trust to belong to an institution that at best turns a blind eye... "**

"I suggest the back entrance, SIR," said the hall porter.

"Under no circumstances. Kindly open the doors and let me out."

"... and at worst secretly enjoys, misogynist tropes such as those this newspaper has repeatedly condemned ... "

"It's more than my job's worth, SIR."

"Don't be absurd."

"Macready's membership overwhelmingly comprises privileged white men ... "

"Sir ... "

"I *am ordering you* to open the doors."

"The resignation from Macready's of all judges, Members of Parliament, bishops and university chancellors ... "

"For crying out loud, man! I will take full responsibility."

The hall porter unlocked the doors and slowly pulled one of them open, creaking loudly, to about a foot's gap. Hector squeezed through and made his way down the slippery stone steps of Macready's Club, holding onto the handrail all the way. Brigit was in full throat—

"It is high time ... "

She stopped mid-proclamation when saw Hector, and marched through the rain towards him. The Channel Four camera crew moved in closer.

"I demand that you give this to your chairman!!"

She pressed her petition against Hector's clenched fists.

"I shall do no such thing."

Hector made to brush past her, but she blocked his way.

"You shall!"

"I certainly shall not."

He grabbed the wet manilla envelope, ripped it in half and threw the pieces into her livid face.

"Bugger off, you ghastly harridan!"

Brigit dropped her megaphone and leaped at him. Claws out. He tried to defend himself by slicing the air between them with his umbrella. Someone in the crowd yelled -

"It's the slave trader!"

Brigit grabbed Hector's umbrella, and they wrestled with it for a few seconds before she lost her footing and fell down the steps, pulling Hector with her. A 'Queers for Palestine' protester broke her fall—but Hector the slave-trader had no such luck. He toppled backwards onto the pavement, cracking his skull on a kerbstone. Rivulets of blood and rainwater trickled into a nearby drain.

Part Two

1. An *extraordinary* general meeting

The members arrive from all directions, alone or in groups of two and three, like rooks flying through the dusk to a roost. On foot, by taxi, by underground and bus, all heading to the same place, all wearing the same gaudy tie. And—astonishing, though it may seem—no one pays much attention to them.

From the Temple and the Law Courts—along Fleet Street and the Strand. From Parliament, the Home Office and the Supreme Court—up Whitehall and the Charing Cross Road. From their houses in Islington to the north, or Kensington and Chelsea to the west. From Canary Wharf in the east and Lambeth in the south. All heading to the same place, all wearing the same gaudy tie.

Consultants from Barts Hospital and St. Thomas's. Landowners from Buckinghamshire, Bedfordshire and Berkshire. Lawyers, actors, writers, politicians, pundits. Chatting about the cases they have won, the books they have written, the roles they have been offered, the malignant tumour they have removed, the malignant MP they have interviewed.

But no matter how fascinating their chatter, no one pays much attention to them—or their gaudy ties.

Things improve when they reach their destination. The theatre has been generously loaned to them for the purposes of the meeting, on the strict understanding that the auditorium will be vacated by seven o'clock (in order to accommodate an audience optimistically expected for a musical adaptation of Strindberg's "The Father"). Reporters mill around the entrance. Cameras flash at the appearance of well-known (and less well-known) faces. Pedestrians gather and watch from a respectful distance

There's xx!

Look! It's yy!

Isn't he in 'Mosquito Man'?

Cab drivers slow down to take a look but pretend not to. They've seen it all before.

Isadora Jarre—feminist, campaigner, sub-editor of *The London Bugle* and relentless critic of Macready's—accosts any celebrity she can recognise; and failing recognition, anyone wearing the Macready tie. She asks them which way they intend to vote. Some linger with her, hoping to attract television coverage. Others bend their heads and hurry past, hoping to avoid it.

Who is this pleasant fellow, ambling towards the theatre? None other than Patrick Rowlands, actor and occasional game-show panellist. He tells Isadora that he wants to hear the competing arguments before deciding how to vote. But he agrees with her, behind a cheeky "*just for your ears*" hand, that it does seem wrong, in the twenty first century, to allow places to which women are refused entry.

James Purdey KC arrives with General Sir Simeon Wallace-Black. They cut Isadora and her impertinent questioning dead.

Hello! There's Lord Justice Justice, surrounded by a bevy of young barristers—who, I emphatically state, are not trying to curry favour with him. They form a protective bait-ball against Isadora's yellow-fin tuna and swim into the theatre unscathed.

The great hulk of Saul Trencherman MP is fair game for Isadora Jarre. But she's no match for him: he '*wants to make it clear, once and for all*' that he only joined the club '*so that he could reform it from the inside*'. What a courageous stance!

Now: that tall, elegant, impeccably dressed and perfectly coiffed beau can only be Quentin Latimer KC. Dripping with charm, he tells Isadora that because her paper had been kind enough to publish his written Opinion in full, it was possible she knew the answer to her question before she asked it. She presses him if he stands by his opinion. He gives her a beatific smile and passes into the theatre.

*

No large assembly that relies on microphones and loudspeakers for communication between dais and floor would be complete without the ear-splitting whine of feedback. Pierre Moreau, the club secretary, takes control of the equipment's testing, bellowing "*Prova, Prova*" into each microphone, in case we should forget he was once secretary of the *Ciocolo delle Teatrale* in Rome.

As the auditorium fills, one by one and in no particular order, members of the house committee cross the temporary bridge over the orchestra pit and take their places in a row of chairs on the stage. The more youthful spirits in the audience (some of them under sixty!) applaud the committee's clumsy entrance.

The stalls are filling near to capacity, with members exchanging greetings and chatting in anticipation of a boisterous meeting.

> *Did you read Isadora Jarre in the Bugle this morning?*
>
> *It's repeated, almost word for word, in the Cornet.*
>
> *She's obsessed!*
>
> *I thought she was spot-on, actually!*
>
> *I thought she was talking crap.*
>
> *She's only saying what the rest of London is thinking.*
>
> *Screw the rest of London!*

An actor-knight, arriving late, makes a good natured scene about being forced to sit in a 'restricted view' seat on the extreme right of the auditorium. Someone shouts-

> *Now you know what it's like for the rest of us!*

To be quite certain that everyone has arrived, Ambrose Harding, in consultation with Lord Justice Justice, takes the decision (but does not communicate it to the members) to wait five minutes past the scheduled start-time before embarking on his opening remarks; during which five minutes no one else turns up, the house committee sits on the stage looking rather foolish, and the audience becomes increasingly restless.

At last, Ambrose gets to his feet, to modest but respectful applause. The instant he begins to speak, the ear-splitting whine of feedback blasts the auditorium—of course it does!—as loud as anything experienced during set-up. Pierre Moreau, not the least self-importantly, strides across the stage to a mixing-desk in the wings, adjusts some dials, and the dreadful noise stops. As a security measure against further technical problems, he remains there for the rest of the meeting.

Ambrose taps his microphone to make the loudspeakers 'pop'—because that is the done thing on these occasions. Then he clears his throat, as he is accustomed to, and begins—

"First of all, I would like to thank everyone for making the effort to come to this important, and indeed *extraordinary*, general meeting. One of the most important, I dare say, in the club's history."

(A chorus of '*hear, hear*')

"And to couple my thanks, as it were, with thanks to Andrew for allowing us to use his theatre."

(Applause)

"May I also extend a warm welcome to those members who, for one reason or another, are not able to make it here personally, but are attending remotely by video link."

The general is on his feet, waving to the usher for a microphone.

"Point of order, chairman."

A tiny voice from the audience squeaks '*Sit down!*'

The general scours the rows of seats to see whom he might court-martial if he could only identify him.

Ambrose consults with Lord Justice Justice. Then -

"Very well, Simeon. But please make it brief. We have limited time."

The general is disinclined to make it brief -

"Will the committee please explain why this is a hybrid meeting? By which I mean that members who are not here in person are allowed to watch and vote on their computers? This was expressly disapproved at our meeting—"

His microphone suddenly cuts out.

(Cries of "*Can't hear you!*" from the audience. Maybe the secretary, anxious that the general's booming delivery should not cause feedback, has accidentally reduced the output volume of the speakers to zero?)

The 'point of order' crackles back on, and then off again, and is ultimately extinguished.

The committee gathers round in a huddle, which breaks when the chairman turns to the audience, and says—

"I will ask JJ to explain the legal advice he has given us." He hands his microphone to the judge. (Happily, Pierre Moreau seems to have resolved the crackling and cut-out problems.)

"Thank you, chairman." says JJ. "I am sure the general could be heard, microphone or no microphone, all the way down Shaftesbury Avenue."

(Sycophantic laughter from some. A discreet finger-in-the-mouth 'vomit' gesture from others.)

"The advice I have given the committee is that the decision to hold a hybrid meeting was circulated to members along with the notification of this meeting under Rule 9(b). The secretary was not served with any notice of objection under rule 11(c)(iii), so the point of order is invalid and cannot be considered."

(Loud mutterings of "*disgraceful*", "*fixed*", "*tin pot*******" (last word inaudible), and "*crooked *****" (last word unrepeatable).

Rival mutterings of "*keep quiet*", "*here we go*", "*misogynist fossils*" and "*oh do shut up*".)

A purple-faced 'status quo' member stands up and splutters: *"A hybrid meeting is no better than a public meeting."* JJ replies: "*I can assure you that the link to this meeting has been sent to members only, in the strictest confidence and under instructions not to share it. Only members of Macready's can see and hear us.*"

Though she is not known to have a sense of humour, the corners of Brigit van der Linden's mouth move almost imperceptibly towards her earlobes when she hears JJ say this—watching the EGM, as she is, from her flat in Red Lion Street.

Isadora Jarre, on the other hand, has not arrived back at the Bugle in time to catch the judge's reassuring words; but the small party gathered around the laptop in her office tells her the joke as soon as she gets there.

Ambrose clears his throat, again, and resumes his introduction:

"As you are aware, Quentin Latimer KC has advised the club that its *unamended* rules already allow women to be proposed and elected as members."

Someone shouts -

No they don't!

Another goes—

Shhhh!

Yet another goes—

51

Shhhhh yourself!

Ambrose continues—

"Your committee, comprising (amongst others), three KCs, two Court of Appeal judges, a Member of Parliament—"

And a Partridge in a pear tree!

(Much laughter.)

"Indeed so," says the chairman. "The house committee, as I was saying, has decided to accept Quentin's advice."

(Hissing and 'tut-tutting'.)

From the darkness—

It wasn't unanimous.

Another voice reminds everyone -

An overwhelming majority of one!

Now the general is on his feet again -
"Point of order, Chairman."
"Oh dear . . . Yes general?"
"How is it that I was able to read the committee's decision in the Bugle, the night before you informed the membership of it?"
"I have no idea. But that is not an issue for discussion tonight."
A member of the audience, stands and demands, loudly—

Why not?

The chairman goes into session with JJ, after which -

"Gentlemen, we *must* move on. We have the theatre until seven o'clock. If you want to raise an issue about the club's affairs being leaked to the press, the rules provide ample process by which to do so."

We will.

You can count on it.

"*Please* may we have no more disruption from the floor?"

A little pause, in acknowledgement of the chairman's authority. Then a stern voice from the stalls -

If I catch the boy who keeps interrupting . . .

(Prolonged laughter.)

"Gentlemen. *Please.*"

The audience settles down. Ambrose continues, wearily -

"As I have already said, the house committee has decided to accept Quentin's advice. Tonight, you are being asked whether you approve that decision or disapprove. I must emphasise, you are not being asked, yourselves to *interpret* the club's rules."

Murmur runs up and down the rows of seats—

Is that so?

Apparently.

I thought that was why we were here.

"There are six speakers whose names have been put forward. Substantial written points of view have been circulated, and I must ask speakers simply to summarise their principal arguments. Because of the strict time-constraints, each of you will have a maximum of three minutes. JJ, I believe you are up first in support of Quentin's advice."

JJ walks to the front of the stage.

"I won't take me three minutes, chairman, because there is only one sensible answer."

Addressing the club's members as he used to address a jury, he speaks to them confidentially, as though there is a tacit understanding between them.

> "Have you ever tossed a coin, to help you decide what to do? If it comes down 'heads' you will do such and such. If it comes down 'tails', you won't. And when it comes down 'tails', have you ever found yourself wishing it had come down 'heads'? The fact is, you should never have flipped the coin in the first place: you should have done what you wanted to, and not let your preference be dictated by the arbitrary spin of a coin.
>
> "We have two rival interpretations to consider: which would you *prefer* to be the one we accept tonight? Which interpretation, if approved by the majority, might you wish had been rejected? Do you want to continue swimming against the tide of public opinion? Do you want to be, and be seen to be, ridiculed for being a member of what the papers are calling '*an anachronistic bastion of inequality that stubbornly refuses to evolve*'?
>
> "Quentin Latimer KC, than whom no one is more eminent or respected, has interpreted our rules as embracing the equality of women; as affirming Macready's commitment to the enlightened principles

of merit, fairness, and progress; as welcoming, rather than spurning, an untapped pool of talent, expertise, and fresh perspectives that can only make Macready's Club a stronger, more vibrant meeting of minds—of *friends,* for heaven's sake—now and for generations to come.

"Do you really want to reject that interpretation? If the coin fell that way, *would you wish it hadn't?*"

The judge returns to his seat. Loud applause. Ambrose says—
"Thank you, JJ. You had me at '*It won't take three minutes.*'"

(The laughter from one half of the members sits unhappily with the sour faces on the other half.)

"Purdey, I have you as next," says Ambrose. "Are you for or against the motion?"

From the auditorium -

Ha ha.

Very funny.

Get on with it.

James Purdey doesn't approach the stage. He remains in the stalls, 'one of the people', and signals to an usher for a microphone. 'Roly Poly' Rowlands slaps him on the back -
"Once more unto the breach, dear friend, once more!"

(A slow handclap while Purdey waits, his head tilting down, his eyes shut.)

The usher weaves his way along a row of seated 'reformers', who a cynic might think were deliberately making his journey difficult. At last, he reaches Purdey, gives him the hand-held microphone, and he is set to go.

He begins with a jovial dig at JJ -

> "What a treat! A Court of Appeal judge has urged us to ignore the law—our rules—and do whatever we want!"

"That is not what I said," mutters JJ, shaking his head.

> "Macready's rules do not expressly limit membership to men. Neither do they expressly extend the offer of membership to women. The rules are silent on the topic, one way or another, because the position is blindingly obvious and has been blindingly obvious for one and a half centuries. Macready's was a club inaugurated by men so they could enjoy the society of other, like-minded men.
>
> "That much *is* expressed in the rules. But it doesn't mean women are banned. 'Banned' is an inappropriate and deliberately inflammatory word, intended to whip up prejudice and dampen rational thought. There is no question of banning women: the club is not *about* women or *for* women. That is not 'banning' them. I am a Norfolk man, and a barrister. But I am not banned from the Norfolk Young Farmers Association. The association is not *about* me, or *for* me. It is about, and for, young farmers.
>
> "You, who I am quite sure understand the position perfectly, are being cajoled into bending the knee to appease the noisome masses who either do not understand, or have set their faces against understanding,

> what Macready's Club is all about: somewhere for us to socialise with other men who have similar interests. As that meerkat in the advert says—'simples'.
>
> "And don't let's forget the law of unintended consequences. If Quentin is correct, and our rules already allow women to be members, it follows that every time we have rejected the proposal of a woman *because she is a woman* (and there have been enough well-publicised instances of that!) we have been acting unlawfully and are vulnerable to a discrimination claim under the Equality Act."

JJ shakes his head again. But in Red Lion Street, Brigit van der Linden makes a careful note.

> "This motion should never have been put to the vote. It is predicated on abject nonsense. It is preposterous, imprudent, and an insult to our intelligence. I urge you to vote against it."

Purdey takes his seat to a sprinkling of applause.

Hear, hear!

Good man!

Next up is the actor-knight in the 'limited visibility' seat. He cannot bring himself to speak from the auditorium and laboriously makes his way across the orchestra pit onto the stage. His sole contribution is to tell the meeting that he recently sat next to a woman who was a guest at the club's centre table, and he had a thoroughly enjoyable evening. He takes all of his three minutes to say so.

Now it is the general's turn. He begins impressively -

"Gentlemen!"

(Long pause.)

"And also, if you are here, the scoundrel who has been leaking the club's private business to the press."

Shame!

Disgraceful!

"That person has forfeited the right to be called a 'gentleman', and the only alternative word that comes to mind is too coarse even for a group of bad-mouthed misogynists such as the Bugle would have us believe we are. What I can say, however, and I say it with no hesitation whatsoever, is ..."

Can't hear you!

The microphone again! What *is* wrong with it? Pierre is at the mixing desk, obviously trying to put the fault right. Desultory bursts of the general's speech are for the most part lost in the crackle of static electricity, save for what sounds like "contemptible", repeated three or four times, and an unmistakable "horsewhipped".

The crackle dies down. A couple of '*provas*' from Pierre, and the general's microphone is live again.

"The issue tonight is not, with respect to the chairman, whether we accept Quentin's *imaginative* opinion ..."

(Some laughter)

"The issue tonight, gentlemen, is whether we allow ourselves to be bullied."

> *Never!*

"Whether by the Bugle newspaper..."

> *Awful rag!*

"By Brigit van der Linden..."

> *Ghastly woman!*

"By a petition signed by one hundred, non-member, virtue-signalling lawyers..."

> *How much did they charge?*

"Or by Baroness thing-me-bob and her Commission for diversity, equality, sugar and spice and all things nice."

(Hearty laughter, and a sense that the general might be carrying the audience with him.)

> "Have the courage, gentlemen, to do what you think is right, not what you think will give you an easy ride on the 'Today' programme, or a film-role, or a cabinet position or judicial appointment."

(With that entreaty the general loses one half of the audience.)

> "Macready's was founded as a gentlemen's club. It has flourished as a gentlemen's club. Long may it remain a gentlemen's club."

(Thunderous applause from the other half.)

Last but one, the chairman invites Saul Trencherman to give the final speech in support of Quentin's advice. The MP remains seated; leaning forward, his forearms on his knees, staring out at the audience, his head moving slowly from side to side as he takes them all in. There is stoney silence. When at last he stands, as though reluctantly and with feigned effort, he walks to the edge of the stage, leans over the orchestra pit and says -

"Bullied?"

He turns ponderously towards the general -

"I know who is doing the bullying around here."

It is the first nakedly hostile note to be sounded between the speakers. He stays—over long—in that menacing position, then swivels round to address the members.

"Macready's is a club that prides itself on patronage of the arts, cultivation of knowledge, and the celebration of accomplishment. Can we, in good conscience, continue to bar from our ranks women who exemplify those very qualities?

"I am holding a list of over two hundred members. Each has written to the chairman saying that if Quentin's opinion is not accepted tonight, they will have no choice but to resign from the club. Each has given me permission to name him if necessary—though I could hardly name them all in three minutes.

"Let me group them under their professions. Actors, Musicians, Writers, Judges, Barristers, Bishops, Doctors, Surgeons, Chancellors, Academics, Diplomates—even some politicians."

The MP smiles ingratiatingly and pauses for an appreciation of his droll humour. But the audience is mute.

> "Those at the peaks of their careers, and those at the foothills. All valued members of Macready's, all writing to the chairman in essentially the same terms: that if we ignore the almost universal clamour of disapproval and continue to exclude women from membership, they will, with great regret and infinite sadness, be forced to resign.
>
> "I should perhaps make it clear that I am one of the two hundred who have written to the chairmen."

"As am I," says Lord Justice Justice, sitting behind him.

"Me too," says silk and rayon.

It is not quite "*I am Spartacus*", but declarations of intent to resign are voiced from here and there and everywhere. Saul Trencherman remains standing until sure he has heard the last of them. Then, without saying another word, he walks imperiously back to his chair.

(Silence.)

Ambrose, coughs, stands, clears his throat and invites the last speaker 'from the floor': Doctor Hans Fleischer, Consultant Psychiatrist at St. Mary Bethlehem, and recently appointed visiting Professor of Psychiatry at St. Dymphna College, Uxbridge University.

Curiously, of all those who speak it is the psychiatrist who 'loses his rag'. He begins in a conciliatory tone:

> "It is a great pity that the differences between those in favour of admitting women and those against have

> been framed as the differences between right and wrong. That is a false dichotomy. Neither side (and there really shouldn't be 'sides') is right, and neither side is wrong."

(This is Dr. Hans's "*I come to bury Caesar*" opening gambit.)

> "There is no 'right and wrong'. No issue of principle. No genuine issue, that is—though it seems to me that 'preference' has sometimes been dressed up as 'principle' as a means to an end."

(Marc Antony took a little longer to back-peddle. But he was not limited to three minutes.)

> "The simple truth is that some prefer a mixed-sexes club, and why shouldn't they? And others prefer a single-sex club, and why shouldn't *they*? I bear those who disagree with me no ill will..."

(For Brutus is an honourable man.)

> "But I regret to say that those of us who would prefer Macready's to remain as it is, a club for gentlemen, have felt the full force of ill-will. We have been called 'Misogynist'—an old favourite. We heard it again tonight. 'Dinosaurs' has been hurled at us ever since this issue was first debated. Only just now, someone shouted 'fossils' at us. Our modest preference for male company, according to the Bugle, is '*disgraceful*' and '*a vice that dare not speak its name*'.
>
> "A vice, gentlemen! Apparently, it is a vice to disagree with them!

"You will forgive me if I fancy myself—"

We know you do, Hans!

"—if I *consider* myself, because I am a psychiatrist, better able than many to withstand the onslaught of incessant, unrelenting abuse."

You need to be, dear!

"But even I have been affected by the torrent of *ad hominem* attacks on Macready's members. And to my certain knowledge so have many others. Far too many, who tell me they have begun to wonder if there is, after all, something odd, something not quite wholesome, about the innocent pleasure they take, from time to time, in the society of other men.

"I recently heard a distinguished jurist say in interview, '*I do not understand what some members of Macready's have to fear about the company of women.*'

"'*Fear*', he said. And this scholar chooses his words carefully. What an insidious seed of self-doubt he deliberately planted there! And when you think of things not merely accepted but celebrated these days! A man may marry another man, and good for him!—but he is odd, very odd, if he wishes to socialise with other men.

"*What does he have to fear?*" goes the jibe, unkind and effective, "*in the company of women?*"

Ambrose Harding cuts in—"You have thirty seconds, Hans." The good doctor picks up speed and raises his voice:

> "There has been a sustained campaign, waged internally as well as externally, on television and in the press—a press, I should add, kept well supplied with ammunition by members of this very club—for the express purpose of making you, who are about to vote, nervous, afraid even, to admit a natural and harmless preference."

The chairman—"Ten seconds".

The visiting professor to Uxbridge University is undaunted—

> "A small caucus within Macready's seems determined to frog-march us to the beat of their drum—not as a matter of principle, so it appears to me, but because they *must* have their own way. I don't believe their motive is any more fine than that. They failed to have their way ten years ago, and the failure has eaten into their better selves."

The chairman says "Thank you, Hans"—pointedly. But Hans will not stop:

> "They *will* have their own way now, *at any cost*, even if it means damaging the reputation of the club and publicly insulting a huge swathe of its members."

Pierre at the mixing desk shrugs a "Shall I?" to JJ, who nods his head.

"Thank you, Hans," says Ambrose. "I have indulged you more than I should. We must move on."

"I have only a few sentences more."

"No. We must move on to the vote."

Hans ignores him -

"Having in mind the means they have employed, the pettiness of their motives, the short-sightedness as to the consequences—which Purdey has touched on—"

Sit down dear!

Give it a rest, Sigmund!

The secretary mutes Hans's microphone, but he shouts—

"I urge you to vote against this motion..."

For Christ's sake Hans, sit down!!

Let him speak!

"...and reject the palpable nonsense underlying it: that a man is a woman, that a woman is a gentleman."

That a cat is a dog!

Yada Yada!

Shut up!

YOU shut up!

If only the English were as fun as the Spanish or French, a fight might break out. Hans is now yelling at the top of his voice -

"The wilful blindness that insists our rules *already* allow women to become members of Macready's. They don't. OF COURSE they don't. You KNOW they don't. It's nonsense. You are being asked to lie, gentlemen. To LIE! Not to *them*..." Hans waves his hand dismissively at the house committee. "... but to yourselves."

Sit down, you old bore!

Resisting the temptation of a Gregory Peck finish—"*For God's sake, do your duty!*"—Hans yields the microphone to an usher.

But the uproar continues.

> *Christ! What an old woman!*
>
> *You <u>want</u> us to lie?*
>
> *Grow up!*
>
> *Where's your sense of honour?*
>
> *Idiot!*
>
> *Coward!*

Ambrose holds his hands to the auditorium, like a cop holding back the traffic:

"Gentlemen! Please! Gentlemen! We have very little time. Please vote on your keypads now. 'Yes' to adopt Quentin's opinion. 'No' to reject it. Those attending remotely have 'yes' or 'no' buttons at the foot of their computer screens."

At the Bugle's headquarters in Wapping, Isadora Jarre experiments, for the sheer hell of it, with a 'yes'. Her vote is accepted, even before Ambrose has said -

"Please vote NOW!"

Isadora hits 'yes' again, and her vote is accepted a second time. She has a third go but receives an 'error' message.

The push-bar doors to old cinemas and theatres are incapable of being opened without a loud crash. The doors to the stalls seats in the theatre are no exception. While the members are still trying to fathom which button means they are in favour of admitting women, and which means they are against, the double-doors from the foyer burst open and Hector Floodgate hobbles in on crutches, his right ankle in plaster, his neck in a brace. The bandage round his head looks like a turban.

Hector!

I thought he was in hospital.

I thought he was dead!

Soon, pretty much every face is turned away from the stage.

Good god!

What's he doing here?

Ambrose Harding tap-taps his microphone. "Gentlemen!"

Christ! He looks awful!

"Gentlemen. Please!"

Tap! Tap! Tap!

"I have the result of the vote."

All interest in Hector is lost. Ambrose clears his throat. He is incapable of making any announcement without doing so—but *this* announcement requires a double-clearance.

"The computer shows that 59.1% are in favour of the motion, and 40.9% are against. The motion is carried."

Some cheering. Some booing. Some swearing. Some applause. The clunk of stalls-seats as the audience makes for the exit. Hector limps out of the theatre before anyone reaches him.

Quentin's opinion has been approved. The club's rules do not need to be amended. Women are (and always have been, so it would seem) eligible to be proposed and elected as members of Macready's Club.

With their heads buried firmly in the sand (and elsewhere), the majority has admitted on the club's behalf that for at least two decades Macready's Club has been unlawfully discriminating against women.

*

The next night, Purdey took his wife to dinner at a side table in Macready's coffee room.

"Possibly for the last time," he said. "Unless, now they've changed the rules, you would like to join?"

"And have to talk to your weird friends? Are you mad? None of us want to *join*! We liked coming to your fuddy-duddy club just the way it was, as your guests. I can't think why that awful Dutch woman was so desperate to ruin everything."

"She, and a few others."

"But why?"

"Why indeed," said Purdey.

He looked around him—at every favourite painting, every familiar face at the centre table, every unfamiliar face making its maiden entrance; at the silver candelabras and the crystal chandeliers; at the great oak doors, the huge sash windows framed by rich red and gold embroidered curtains; at the waiters with their steaming trays, the sommelier giving his quiet, almost confidential recommendations, the laden dessert trolly making its squeaky-wheeled way from table to table—and he raised his glass, as though toasting the whole room, the whole club: "*Fin de siècle*," he said.

"*Fin de siècle*, darling. It was lovely while we had it, though, wasn't it?"

2. All About Hector

When Hector was carried away in an ambulance, the house committee did not know if he was alive or dead. Neither did most of the demonstrators in the street below, who scattered when they saw blood pouring from his skull. Only the club's hall porter, who had called for the ambulance and waited in the rain for it to arrive, the press, Brigit, and one of the female barristers (who, in her soaking wet wig and gown, looked like a giant pot-scourer) saw that the unconscious Hector was still breathing.

Up in the committee room, Ambrose being satisfied that things were under control below, and being disinclined to get caught on Channel 4's cameras, he suggested that the meeting should be brought to a speedy conclusion, and that anyone leaving the club should use the back exit.

Three hasty decisions were made before the meeting was formally closed. Firstly, that in the circumstances it would be inappropriate to 'post' Hector's expulsion on the members' notice board—which ordinarily the secretary would have done immediately on conclusion of the meeting. Secondly, that further consideration of Hector's coffee room felony should be postponed until they knew how he was, and—if he were alive—what was the prognosis for his recovery. Thirdly, and without any meaningful discussion, Quentin's written Opinion—that the unamended the rules of the club allowed women to be elected—was adopted (by a majority of one), subject to confirmation by the members at an extraordinary general meeting to be held as soon as practicable. As we have seen, that meeting took place and Quentin's opinion was duly confirmed.

*

It had been thought that Hector was still in hospital, 'critical but stable', until his dramatic appearance at the back of the auditorium demonstrated the contrary. So when the house committee next convened, it was understandable that the first item on their agenda raised the delicate issue of how to handle his expulsion.

"We can't go ahead and announce it right now," said Ambrose. "It would look unfeeling. You saw the state he was in."

"It would *be* unfeeling. It would *look* callous," said Dr. Fleischer.

"I could not disagree more strongly," said JJ. "We made a unanimous decision. It was minuted. The only reason it was not posted was on compassionate grounds. As I see it, Hector has exhausted all the compassion he may be thought entitled to, even by the most generous of us. Now he's up and about, and showing his impudent face where he pleases, including in this club, I can see no valid reason not to put our decision to immediate effect."

"There is this valid reason, *perhaps*," said Dr. Fleischer. "I was concerned at the time and maybe I should have voiced my concerns then. But I do so now. I fear we may have been too hasty in our decision to expel young Hector."

(An explosion from the judge, to describe which adequately, the English language has yet to invent words.)

"I think we should keep an open mind as to whether his conduct can be explained by reasons other than calculated insolence. That's all I am suggesting."

"It was calculated and sustained insubordination!" said JJ.

"A textbook case of 'conduct unbecoming a gentleman'," added Saul Trencherman.

"You may be right, of course, but I am far from sure. His behaviour, not just when he was asked to apologise to JJ for his outburst in the coffee room, but more generally—his absurd proposal for amending the rules for instance."

"The penis proposal!" said JJ.

"You make it sound like a John Grisham novel," said Quentin.

Ambrose confessed that he had always suspected it was Hector who pinned the handwritten note under Lord Pugh's letter of resignation.

"Of course it was him!" said JJ.

"I have watched Hector closely, in the bar, over dinner," said Ambrose. "I don't know, I'm a businessman not a psychiatrist...but it seems to me that he might have what are fashionably called 'mental health issues'."

"That is my point," said Dr. Fleischer.

"Stuff and nonsense," spluttered the judge.

"Mental health issues are a 'get out of jail free' card these days," chimed silk and rayon. But no one was sure whether that meant he was with JJ or with Dr. Fleischer.

"I agree with Hans," said Quentin. "Albeit with some reluctance. I think it is highly desirable, if not imperative that we procced with a measure of caution. If Hector is—how shall I put it? Don't minute this Pierre—*suffering in that way*, whether due to the stress of the seismic changes the club is undergoing or for other, more personal reasons, it would be prudent not to do anything in haste that we might come to regret later. If, for example, we should find ourselves on the receiving end of litigation."

"Which Hector, of all people, would delight in bringing," said Saul.

"I *have* been worried about him, if I'm honest," said Ambrose. "Sometimes, his behaviour does seem...well, a little..."

"Off the rails," said Pierre.

"Balderdash!" said JJ. "He's as sane as any of us."

"Maybe so," replied Dr. Fleischer. "Maybe so. But on any view, it's a delicate matter. I propose we put our final decision on hold, certainly until we are sure Hector is fully recovered. Ya? And we can monitor his behaviour in the meantime."

Murmurs of "I agree", "hear, hear", and "that has to be right", made it unnecessary to take a vote. But JJ insisted it be placed in the minutes that he disagreed.

"Do we tell him he is on probation?" asked the secretary.

"No!" said the judge. "Give him enough rope to hang himself."

"If you haven't already saved him the trouble," said Ambrose.

*

Hector had no idea that a Sword of Damocles called "expulsion" was dangling over his head, suspended by a single strand of horsehair called "good behaviour". If he had known he was on probation, he might not have carried out—but there again he might have!—the stunts he decided to pull next.

First, he put his Macready ties up for sale on eBay, under "Women's Accessories". The amusement and outrage of his friends and enemies were in equal measure, and short-lived.

Then, even before the eBay joke had run its course, he took out an advertisement in as many of the London newspapers as would take it, appealing for asylum to be given to disaffected members of Macready's.

The London

Monday, May 11, 2023

URGENT APPEAL

Following the invasion of Macready's Club by women, literally dozens of vanquished members have been forced to try to find asylum elsewhere. Unscrupulous traffickers are demanding large sums of money, directing the displaced though Soho and across the perilous terrain known as 'Leicester Square', unescorted with just an A to Z to guide them, in the hope of joining one the idyllic clubs in St. James's and Pall Mall. But not everyone makes it. Only last week, a group of six asylum-seekers was found stranded in Soho House.

THE DILEMMA Some of the promised clubs are not safe. Identifying 'safe' clubs is no longer the straightforward task that it used to be. The fall of Sprats illustrates how easily what might have been regarded as safe a year ago cannot be taken for granted as safe today.

WON'T YOU HELP? We desperately need to find safe clubs for those migrants. Please send suggestions to HectorFloodgate@Gmail

No club is too small

If that were not enough for the house committee to find him in breach of probation, the third, and in the event the most damaging of Hector's pranks, was to hold a memorial service for Macready's Club at St. Peter's Church, Soho.

So as not to arouse suspicion and risk the church's refusal of the booking, Hector compiled a traditional, if somewhat dull, Order of Service, and included it with his written application.

> The departed was Johannes Dough (1957-2023).
>
> The congregation would take their seats to the sound of Purcell's 'Music for the Funeral of Queen Mary'.
>
> The opening blessing was the standard "*Almighty God, we rejoice in your promise of love, joy and peace.*"
>
> The readings were Matthew 11:28 (*Come to me, all who travail and are heavy laden*); and John 14:1-3 (*Do not let your hearts be troubled*).
>
> The hymns were "*Dear Lord and Father of mankind*" and "*Abide with me*".
>
> The Eulogy was to be given by Lieutenant General Sir Simeon Wallace-Black, KBE, CB.

The Parochial Church Council of The Ecclesiastical Parish of St Peter, Soho gave its blessing to the Order of Service and accepted the booking (and fee of fifteen hundred pounds) without demur. They were unaware, of course, that Hector had compiled an alternative Order of Service, rather different from the one approved by the Church Council, which would not be circulated in advance but be handed to the carefully chosen 'mourners' as they crossed the threshold of the church and entered the vestibule.

All reasonable steps were taken to minimise the attendance of strangers. The event was not publicised. Martin would assume the duties of Officiant — he being an ordained priest — therefore the Rector could politely be excused his attendance. A professor of keyboard studies at the Royal College of Music, and *status quo* member of Macready's, was acknowledged by the Parochial Council as of sufficient competence to play the church's grand old Henry Bevington organ — so the church's resident organist could likewise be released.

Two down, and only one to go — the Verger. But it proved more difficult to be rid of him. He alone held the keys, and he alone could unlock the doors. Furthermore, he was adamant that he '*would not countenance*' abandoning to a stranger his duties to prepare the church and welcome the congregation.

Having no choice but to make the best of it, Hector trusted that the Verger had seen a thousand memorial services and hoped he wouldn't pay particular attention to this one.

A forlorn hope, as things turned out.

3. What Brigit did next

If it would be preposterous to describe Brigit van der Linden as gracious in defeat, it would stretch the limits of credibility to praise her as magnanimous in victory.

The morning after securing the historic vote at Macready's EGM (as she would have it, single-handedly), she took a photograph of a female pupil barrister, in wig and gown, standing on the first of the eight or so stone steps leading to Macready's great iron gates—which she ensured, by having the photo-shoot at 6:00 am, were symbolically closed.

The photograph on the front page of the Bugle carried the caption: "**First step on the stoney path to Equality**."

The opinion piece printed under the photograph read—

> **We are glad to see that Macready's Club has accepted—kicking and screaming though it may be—that closing its doors to women members is an affront to Diversity, Equality and Inclusion, and that it has been guilty of unlawful discrimination under the Equality Act for at least two decades. But obtaining that long-overdue confession is but the first step on an arduous journey. We, and all right-thinking people, must not be beguiled into giving up the fight.**
>
> **This newspaper is proud to have been in the vanguard of ensuring that Macready's fortifications against women are breached, definitively and permanently. We have succeeded, but that is not enough. Foreseeing the inevitability of last night's victory, we recently demanded that "*proposals of women as candidates for membership of Macready's***

are given immediate precedence over the weary list of male supplicants currently waiting to be elected. Only when there is an even split of men and women members will the sins of Macready's past be absolved."

We stand by that demand. If the volte-face we forced on Macready's is not to become mere tokenism, or self-serving virtue-signalling, it is imperative that no time is lost, and the appalling insult to those whose applications for membership have, over the last twenty years or so, routinely been rejected *because they are women*, is acknowledged and compensated by the immediate election of them as members. If not, by civil proceedings or a voluntary settlement in lieu.

We wait with interest to hear what action is being taken to redress Macready's years of unlawful sexism. The club should take heed. The battle is not over. We have not retreated to our tents.

It has been written of Ibsen that he used to keep a scorpion in a glass jar on his desk. Every now and then, when the scorpion appeared to be sick, Ibsen would drop a plum or sugar-lump into the jar, which the scorpion would furiously sting until it had rid itself of all its poison and was, to all appearances, relieved of its sickness. Ibsen likened the writing of his plays to a curative release of his own internal poisons.

Brigit was undoubtedly a species of scorpion, but injecting her toxins into Macready's gave her no peace. More than satisfied with her front-page battle cry in the Bugle, but still hankering to do Macready's harm, she garnered the support of a motley collection of feminists, self-publicists (male and female), holier-than-thou idealists, and a miscellany of obscure academics with a string of qualifications after their names. Then she appended their signatures to an 'open letter' which she sent to every club in London that maintained a 'gentlemen only' membership policy.

It would be tedious to cite even a sentence from the letter, because it comprised the same old demands, in the same old angry language, and the same old threat that if those clubs did not change their ways, *without delay,* Brigit the scorpion would be after them, her sting arched over her back, dripping with deadly venom.

4. National Treasures

The letter that Ambrose read to the House Committee was from the chairmen of six London clubs, each known to maintain a strict 'gentlemen only' membership policy. It was short and to the point:

> *Dear Chairman,*
>
> *Macready's Club has opened a Pandora's Box. We trust that you, your committee, and your members factored-in to your recent decision that certain consequences would necessarily follow. This is to give you formal notice that all reciprocal arrangements between Macready's Club and the clubs listed below, of which we have the honour to be chairmen, are hereby ended.*
>
> Blacks, The Wayfarers, The Lambchop, Jimmy's, Stags, The Surf Club
>
> *Yours, etc.*

"I didn't see that one coming," said silk and rayon.

Pierre Moreau was anxious that the committee should know that he, too, had received a letter, along broadly similar lines, which '*he would like to read aloud with the chairman's permission?*' Ambrose nodded his consent.

"It is addressed to me, as secretary," said Pierre.

"More importantly, who is it *from?*" asked Saul Trencherman, leaning back in his chair, hands cupped behind his head, looking at the ceiling.

Pierre had to confess it was not signed, which to his chagrin diminished its (and his) status somewhat.

"It says—

To the White Feather Club (formerly known as Macready's):

Well bloody done. Have you any idea the chain of events you have set in motion? Virtue-signalling, muppets! When this chicken comes home to roost, I hope it bites you where you ought to have balls.

"Oh dear," said Ambrose. "Well, there we are. Does anyone else have a letter they would like to share? I do hope not."

JJ cut in with the authority he had gained since securing the "yes" vote at the EGM.

"It is essential that we do not let this project lose momentum."

"Project?" queried Dr. Fleischer.

"I think you know what I mean."

Pierre informed the meeting that he had received over one hundred proposals of women, and they were *already* in the candidates' book.

"No, no," said JJ. "The standard procedure takes far too long. We need a gesture. Now. I propose we invite some prominent women, say three of them, to become members at once. We bye-pass the candidates' committee and elect them ourselves, by the power invested in us as trustees."

"Assuming our invitations are accepted," said the general.

"They will be," said Saul.

"I agree with JJ," said Quentin. "The vote at the EGM needs to be consolidated by *action*. The sooner we get some ladies in, the better."

"The Bugle printed a list of distinguished women who they say *should* be members," said Saul. "I'll dig it out.".

Ambrose said he hoped the rapid election of women, *any women*, might placate Brigit van der Linden.

"Nothing will placate Brigit van der Linden," said JJ.

"What we need are 'national treasures'", said silk and rayon enthusiastically.

Quentin suggested the Elgin Marbles.

"How about a much loved actress," said Saul.

"That's a 'given', surely?" said Ambrose.

"And an academic," said Saul. "There's a television historian—you'll know her: a sort of female Kenneth Clarke—I can't remember her name, but I think she was on the Bugle's list."

"Her then," said Quentin, having given the suggestion all the careful consideration required of it.

"And one of those TV cooks?" suggested silk and rayon.

"Ready, steady—you're elected!" said Quentin.

"Definitely not!" snapped JJ.

"They're national treasures."

"That is immaterial."

"OK then, what about a self-made baroness."

"House of Lords by day, BBC by night?" said Quentin.

"Yes. They're very popular."

"Beacons for female aspiration," said Saul Trencherman MP, experimenting with the language for his next television interview.

"May I suggest a sub-committee?" said Ambrose, putting an end to the 'national treasures' tombola. "Saul and Quentin perhaps? If you could sift through the possibles and come up with a shortlist and maybe three recommendations, I will send the invitations as soon as practicable. Do you think you could accomplish that by tomorrow?"

"We can only try," said Quentin.

*

That night, Ambrose composed a letter—

Dear ****,

It is with the greatest possible pleasure that I write on behalf of the trustees of Macready's Club to invite you to become one of three founding lady members, who would be the first such members in the Club's one hundred and fifty years' history.

I know I speak on behalf of all of us in Macready's when I say that not only would we be extremely honoured if you joined us, but your very association and hopefully your presence from time to time would enrich the club in ways beyond description or value.

I do hope you will feel able to accept our invitation. To mark this momentous occasion, the trustees propose that you should become honorary life-members forthwith, relieved of any initial fee or annual subscription.

The following morning, the 'National Treasures Sub-Committee' presented Ambrose with its recommendations:

- **Dame May Kemble**—actress.

- **Professor Ayana Nkosi**—historian and presenter of the award-winning series "Ignoble Histories".

- **Baroness Lovelace**—broadcaster, founder and CEO of Belladonna, an internationally renowned dietary supplement business, focused on women's health.

The letters were delivered by courier that afternoon.

5. In Memoriam

The memorial service for Macready's Club was scheduled for three o'clock in the afternoon, and it was a tedious morning for all concerned to while away the hours before the big event.

Martin passed the time trying on different permutations of his liturgical vestments. It was near lunchtime before he settled on a lightweight, full-length black cassock and black silk chasuble.

Purdey made several attempts at drafting an advice as to the chances of success in an action for nuisance and harassment brought by Greenwich Council against an ice-cream vendor, who had been refused a street trading licence and in revenge drove his van back and forth past the council offices, playing Brahms' Lullaby at full volume. Purdey gave up mid-morning, his mind distracted in anticipation of the afternoon's fun and games and by the tinkling refrain of Brahms' Lullaby played on an ice-cream van.

Hector had an early appointment at the Chelsea and Westminster for the removal of his bandage and neck-brace. He then returned to his house in Kynance Mews, still on crutches, to finalise the 'alternative' Order of Service which he had planned for distribution at the church doors. When he was content with how it looked on screen, he printed a copy to see how it looked on paper.

"*And he saw what he had made, and behold, it was very good.*"

Happy with the fruits of his labours, Hector emailed a copy to anyone with a speaking part and gave the necessary instruction to his computer for the printing of ten further copies. But it was apparent by the third page of the first of them, that his printer had run out of ink.

There were many options for the solution to this minor set-back, but Hector derived a singular pleasure from choosing to have Macready's Club itself provide him with the assistance he needed. So he took a taxi, struggled up those fateful stone steps and made his way to the secretary's office.

Had he known he was under probation and dicing with expulsion, and had he cared whether the secretary liked him or not, he might have paid more attention to the frosty reception he received from Pierre.

"Yes? What is it?"

"I need to borrow the photocopier, if I may."

"You want to take it away?"

"Don't be absurd. I would like to make some copies."

"It is 20p per sheet."

"I think I can manage that. May I?"

The secretary said "You know where it is" in as off-hand a way as is possible and pretended to read the day's correspondence.

Hector went to a little ante room where the photocopier was housed and retrieved the alternative 'Order of Service' from the inside pocket of his jacket. One by one, he smoothed out the pages on the glass pane of the machine, lowered the lid, and made ten copies of each.

The reader may have guessed that there would be little point in detailing this otherwise humdrum sequence of events, if Hector hadn't accidentally left every page of the originals by the side of the photocopier when he picked up the copies.

He casually dropped a ten-pound note on Pierre's desk and returned to his mews house to dress for the Memorial Service.

*

Martin was the first to arrive at St. Peter's, to meet—and hopefully to distract—the Verger. In his ankle-length cassock and flowing silk chasuble, Martin glided towards the church as though floating on air, like a seraph with his wings tucked in.

He was intrigued to see Macready's secretary waiting with the Verger outside the ominously shut entrance. Curiosity turned to alarm when he saw that Pierre was holding Hector's 'Order of Service'.

"*Are you any part of this?*" demanded the livid secretary, waving it at Martin as he arrived.

Without stopping, Martin said "*Bless you, my son*", pirouetted like a spinning top, and retreated in the direction from which he had come, perhaps a little faster than when he arrived, with the Verger shouting after him "*I have been cruelly deceived*".

He hailed the first black cab he saw. It pulled up alongside him but was occupied. The door opened and one of Hector's crutches slammed onto the pavement.

"Get back in!" said Martin.

"What?"

"Get in. Just do it."

Now Pierre was running towards them.

"You sir! Come back here!"

"Let me in, for God's sake," shouted Martin, to the bemusement of a passing group of Japanese tourists, who began filming the incident on their Smartphones.

The crutch retreated into the taxi and Martin followed it. After a few frantic seconds, in which instructions and some paper money were given to the driver, the cab pulled away, tires squealing.

The next winter, back in Sapporo, the Japanese liked to show their videos at *après ski* fondue parties, as proof positive that they were not making it up but had actually witnessed a church in London being robbed by a man dressed as a monk.

*

Thank heavens for the mobile phone! The rest of the invited congregation was quickly diverted to the Wayfarers Club, so that no-one else was ambushed as Martin had been.

The upper morning room was already secured for drinks after the service, and Hector and Martin took immediate possession of it. Six bottles of vintage Krug were put on ice, and Hector asked that a further dozen, all at his expense, were chilled in readiness.

One by one, the displaced St. Peter's congregation turned up at the Wayfarers Club, exhilarated by the narrow escape they had had, and eager for something by way of an entertaining climax. With which, many thought, they were amply rewarded when they were handed Hector's 'Order of Service':

In Loving Memory of
Macready's Club
1873-2023

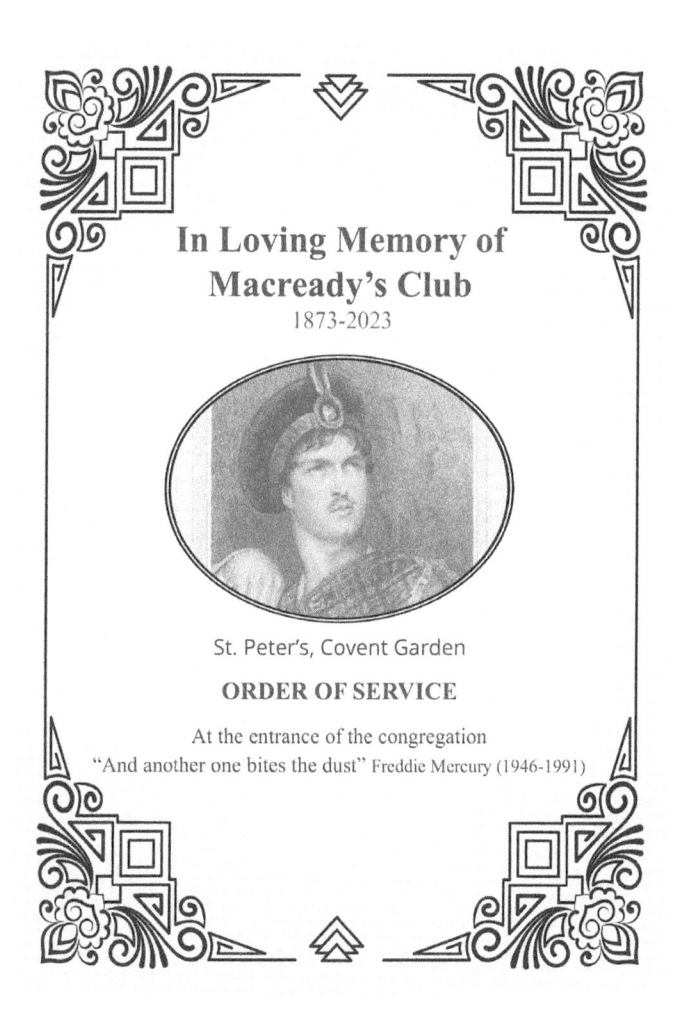

St. Peter's, Covent Garden

ORDER OF SERVICE

At the entrance of the congregation
"And another one bites the dust" Freddie Mercury (1946-1991)

Opening Blessing

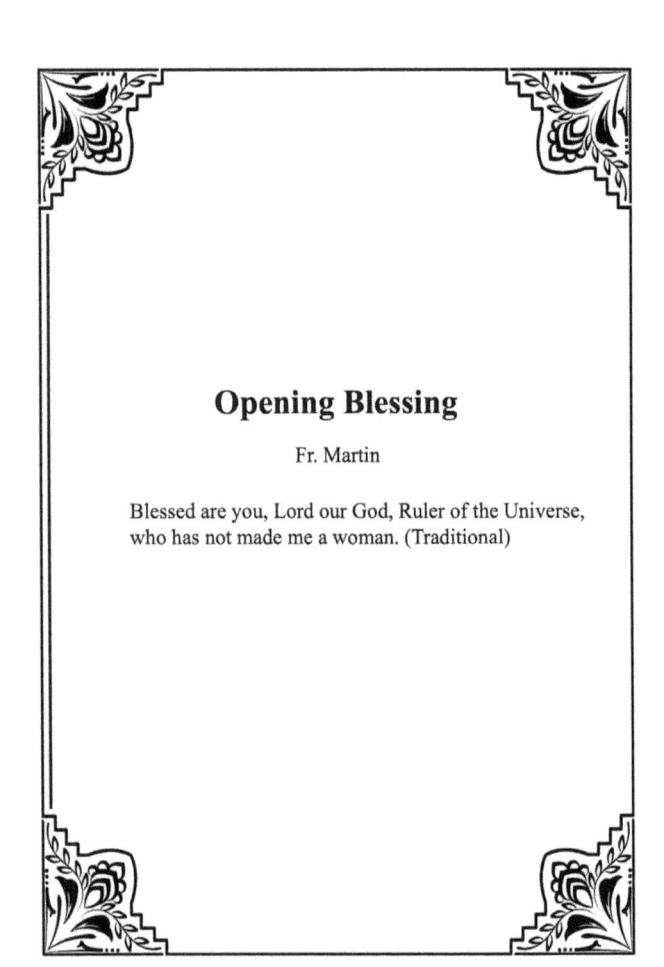

Fr. Martin

Blessed are you, Lord our God, Ruler of the Universe, who has not made me a woman. (Traditional)

Reading – Timothy 22:8-15
General Sir Simeon Wallace-Black

Therefore, I want the men everywhere to pray, lifting up holy hands without anger or disputing.

I also want the women to dress modestly, with decency and propriety, adorning themselves, not with elaborate hairstyles or gold or pearls or expensive clothes but with good deeds, appropriate for women who profess to worship God.

A woman should learn in quietness and full submissions.I do not permit a woman to teach or to assume authority over a man; she must be quiet.

For Adam was formed first then Eve. And Adam was not the one deceived; it was the woman who was deceived and became a sinner.

But women will be saved through childbearing if they continue in faith, love and holiness with propriety.

Hymn

Dear Lord and Father of mankind
Forgive their foolish ways
Macready's Club has lost its mind
And half its members have resigned
In hope of happier days
In hope of happier days
Drop Thy still dews of quietness
Reduce our annual subs
Take from our souls the strain and stress
And let our new-found lives confess
The joys of other clubs
The joys of other clubs

Reading – Paradise Lost
(John Milton: 1608-1674)
Doctor Hans Fleischer

O Eve, in evil hour thou didst give ear To that false worm, of whomsoever taught To counterfeit Man's voice. True in our fall, False in our promised rising. Since our eyes opened, we find indeed, find we know both good and evil: Good lost, and Evil got.

Bad fruit of knowledge, if this be to know, Which leaves us naked thus, of honour void, Of innocence, of faith, of purity, Our wonted ornaments now soiled and stained, And in our faces evident the signs Of foul concupiscence.

Eulogy

The Hon. Hector Floodgate

I first met Macready's Club when I was twenty one years of age and taken to dinner there by my godfather. It was a few years before I was lucky enough to be elected as a member and I proudly took my godfather there as my first guest. Macready's has been a very special place for me ever since: a refuge, a haven. My heart is too full at its passing for me to continue without embarrassing myself.

All I will say is 'Goodbye, dear friend. May you rest in peace'.

Reading – Ephesians
5: 21-23
James Purdey KC

Wives, submit yourselves to your own husbands as you do to the Lord. For the husband is the head of the wife as Christ is the head of the church, his body, of which he is the Savior. Now as the church submits to Christ, so also wives should submit to their husbands in everything.

Hymn

Abide with me, fast flows the cont'ry tide
The chasm deepens, Lord with me abide
When judges quit and famous actors flee
Thou who are not far behind, abide with me.

Swift to its close ekes out my tempr'ry stay
To pastures new, I take myself away
Change and decay in all around I see
O, club that changeth not, abide with me.

I fear no foe, with Thee at hand to bless
Ills have no weight, Opinions even less
Death, where's thy Sting? I fear not Stephen Fry.
I'll lead the way, if Thou abide with me.

Final Blessing

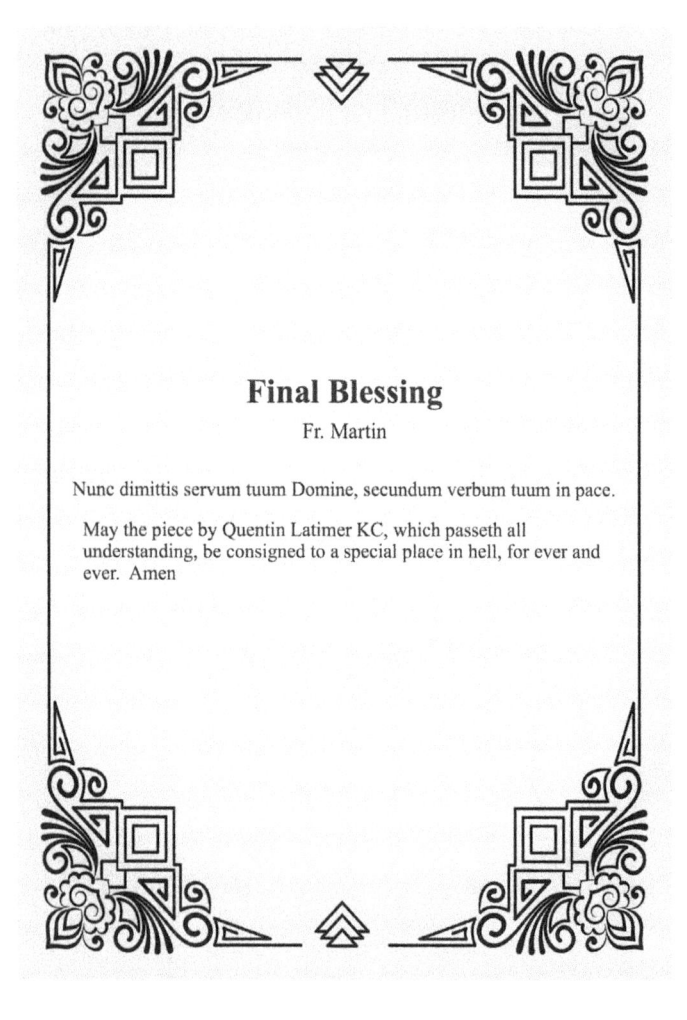

Fr. Martin

Nunc dimittis servum tuum Domine, secundum verbum tuum in pace.

May the piece by Quentin Latimer KC, which passeth all understanding, be consigned to a special place in hell, for ever and ever. Amen

They gathered round the club's boudoir grand piano—the pride of the chairman, but in truth a very mediocre instrument—and each took his role in the Service; the readers proclaiming their Bible extracts with religious fervour, and the congregation singing their hymns lustily.

At the sound of singing, (and possibly at the sight of the club's servants carrying decanters of port and brandy up the stairs to the morning room), various members drifted in to see what was going on, and seeing it, joined in the singing. By early evening there was an enthusiastic throng who insisted the entire Memorial be repeated from scratch. Hector was dispatched to print further copies of the Order of Service—and then again, more copies still.

After a boisterous supper in the coffee room, an eager contingent of Wayfarers demanded a repeat performance of the whole thing; but it degenerated into singing the hymns only, and repeatedly; with one drunken member, not quite sure of the time or place, singing the words of 'Rudolph the Red Nosed Reindeer' to the music of each hymn.

Some lit their cigars in the smoking room. Others, law-abiding citizens, slipped into the Wayfarers' gardens, to enjoy their *Romeo y Julieta* in that narrow window of warmth that an English summer can, at its best, lend to a June night.

*

At the same time as bereft mourners at the Wayfarers Club summoned up remembrance of things past, the secretary of Macready's Club summoned a quorate house committee to decide the fate of Hector Floodgate, in light of his latest 'appalling behaviour'.

In no longer than the three minutes in which members had been permitted to speak at the fateful EGM in a desperate attempt to save their club, Hector's expulsion was confirmed with immediate effect. Pierre Moreau took it upon himself, at once, to 'post' it on the members' notice board, and to post (in the ordinary sense, and first-class) a letter so informing him.

*

By 1:00 am there were only Purdey and Hector left in the gardens of the Wayfarers Club on that balmy summer's evening. They had relived and laughed about the day's events, over and over, and agonised about the possible consequences, until there was nothing left to say; and there were long gaps in their conversation while they smoked their cigars and listened to a blackbird singing, like Paul McCartney's, in the dead of the night.

Hector suddenly broke the silence -

"Look! Over there! It's Brigit van der Linden!"

"Where?

"Over there! By the shrubbery!"

And 'over there' was a splendid brown fox, stock still and staring at them defiantly, as if to say: "*When I move it will be because I decide to, not because I am afraid of you.*"

Purdey imitated the sound of a hunting horn, and the fox looked at him in utter contempt before loping off towards Carlton House Terrace.

"Do you think she's after us?"

"The fox?"

"Brigit."

"She's after *all* of us."

"Why, do you think?

Hector didn't reply.

After a long pause . . .

"God! I love this garden!" he said, lounging back in his chair.

"If I resigned from Macready's, would you put me up for membership?" said Purdey.

"Of course, old thing. But don't resign."

A voice from the darkness of a bedroom window high above them complained that *'people were trying to sleep.'*

"We'd better go in— *Whoah*! Steady there!"

Purdey helped Hector out of his chair and up the few steps leading to the smoking room.

"I think you've had one too many, my dear!"

"I think I have had a half-case too many."

They agreed to meet very soon for lunch.

"I wonder how much trouble we're in," said Purdey.

"It was worth it though, wasn't it?"

"Definitely."

Hector said he didn't think he could make it back to his house in the state he was, and he negotiated with the hall porter for overnight accommodation. Purdey left in search of a cab.

*

The next morning, a cleaner found Hector dead on the floor of his bedroom, still dressed, and with the hint of a smile on his face.

The coroner said it was a delayed lethal pulmonary air embolism, likely to be consequent on the blow to his skull when he fell down the steps of Macready's Club, the night of Brigit's demonstration.

6. Offer and Acceptance

Although the house committee had met expressly to be updated on the proposed election of three ladies as members of Macready's Club, Hector's recent and unexpected death took a temporary precedence over the typed agenda.

Pierre had removed the notice of Hector's expulsion immediately on hearing the news, and the issue under discussion was whether a customary, black-edged expression of the house committee's regret that he had died, should be posted in its place.

"It does seem rather hypocritical," said Ambrose. "First we tell everyone we have chucked him out, then we say how sorry we are that he's no longer with us."

"The notice of expulsion was up for less than twenty four hours," said the secretary.

"But enough of us read it," said Saul Trencherman.

Lord Justice Justice summarised the position as though he were delivering a judgment of the Court of Appeal.

"The custom is and, as I understand it, has always been, that the club will give notice of the death of *a member* on the members' notice board. Hector Floodgate was not a member when he died. He had been expelled for nearly two months. We do not, so far as I am aware, take it upon ourselves to express our regret at the deaths of non-members."

The judge then added—and may God forgive him!—"Even when there *is* regret."

"This too," said Quentin quickly. "His having died in a bedroom of the Wayfarers Club is the talk of the day. Surely it is artificial, if not wholly unnecessary, to 'inform' members of what they know already. And I agree, it would open us up to accusations of rank hypocrisy."

Saul Trencherman also agreed. As did silk and rayon, albeit a little uncertain if it meant he was in favour of a *"House Committee Regrets"* notice or against it.

It was therefore settled that the Hon. Hector Floodgate should be expunged from the consciousness of Macready's Club without further ceremony.

"It is probably for the best," said Ambrose.

The judge cleaned the lenses of his glasses and said nothing.

"And so, to the more pleasant business before us tonight," said Ambrose. "I have received a charming letter, jointly signed by Dame May Kemble, Professor Ayana Nkosi, and Baroness Lovelace. I am pleased to tell you that they have accepted our offer, subject only to one condition."

"A condition?"

"I'll read the letter," said Ambrose.

> *Dear Ambrose, and distinguished members of the House Committee of Macready's Club, whom we have yet to have the pleasure of meeting and knowing by name.*

"They're going to be fun over dinner!" said the general.

> *We hope that you will allow us to speak with one voice…*

"I don't see that lasting."

> *…in expressing our delight in accepting your kind offer of membership of Macready's. We have one concern, however, and must make it a condition of our acceptance, that we should not be honorary members, but ordinary members, subject to the same initial joining fee and annual subscription as the men are subject. We would not want to be, and are sure you would not want us to*

be, regarded as merely token members elected to appease a hostile press.

In the confidence that your committee will understand and agree with our concerns in that regard, we look forward to receiving the honour of membership of Macready's Club and await your instruction as to the next steps in the process.

"What a weird letter," said Quentin.

"But I can see where they are coming from," said Dr. Fleischer.

Ambrose asked if there was any objection to the ladies' proposal.

"It will put more loot in our coffers," said silk and rayon.

"At the same time, we must, and I mean 'must', whatever they say, mark the occasion properly," said Saul. "It is far too special to be allowed to slip by as if of no significance. We have been publicly criticised, and we must put up a public show in response. I propose a grand Club Dinner, black tie, at which the house committee presents the ladies to the members."

"*Proudly* presents," said Ambrose.

"It will be an historic occasion," said Pierre, looking forward to adding it to his CV.

"I hope that whoever leaked all the bad news to the papers has the sense to leak some good news at last," said JJ, without looking at Quentin.

"They will talk about it for years to come," said Pierre.

"Will you draft something for me to send to the ladies?" said Ambrose.

"Should it be to all three jointly, or to each individually?"

"To each individually."

Ambrose duly wrote to each of the three national treasures, saying that he understood their concerns and that the club would of course respect them. But he hoped they would agree to being guests of honour at a dinner to mark the historic occasion, the proposals for which he summarised.

At the next meeting of the house committee, he read the ladies' individual replies: they were in identical terms.

> *Dear Ambrose,*
>
> *Thank you for your letter. Whilst I fully appreciate the significance of the occasion and would accept some departure from the norm as appropriate — and a Club Dinner is of course acceptable — I do not like (and I have spoken to the others, and we are agreed) the idea of being 'presented' to the members. I think we should walk into the Coffee Room <u>as members</u> entitled to do so and take our seats <u>as members</u> — not as a spectacle for the gratification of the men.*
>
> *Dame May has reminded us of Cleopatra's disinclination to be paraded before Rome; and whilst we would be slow to call the male membership of Macready's 'saucy lictors', it is difficult to rid our minds of the awful image she conjured up.*
>
> *Speeches are an unavoidable necessity, we understand that. But perhaps they may be limited to one from you, and one from each of us?*
>
> *Kind regards...*

Ambrose replied to them, individually, saying that he was sure they would reach agreement as to the fine-tuning of the event—which in due course they did.

Two other letters are worth mentioning. Both were addressed to Pierre and were received a couple of weeks before the grand dinner. The first was from Baroness Lovelace:

> *Dear Pierre,*
>
> *There is bound to be considerable public interest in our forthcoming dinner. Do you think a joint press release would be helpful? Please send me your suggestions.*
>
> *Emily Lovelace*

The other was from Professor Nkosi:

> *Dear Secretary,*
>
> *I have heard that there are two vacancies to be filled on the House Committee. Can you let me know the last date for nominations?*
>
> *Yours sincerely,*
>
> *Professor Ayana Nkosi, OBE, MA (Berkeley)*

7. An historic occasion

The three ladies had made no secret that they would have *preferred* their first appearance as members of Macready's to have been as low-key and unexceptional as possible. No fuss. No speeches. No reserved table. They would very much have *liked*, they said, to have made an understated entrance in the coffee room, taken the first available place at the centre table, and submitted to pot-luck as to who came and sat next to them. "*That's what the men have done for the last one hundred and fifty years, and that's what we would have preferred to do in 2023.*"

They understood and sympathised, however, how dearly the club wanted to mark the historic occasion; and they were loath to appear graceless in resisting the splendid welcome that the trustees appeared to have their hearts set on giving them.

"I suppose we must go with the flow," said May Kemble, "however horrid the flow may be."

"It would seem rather ungrateful not to," added Emily Lovelace.

Accordingly, and in the spirit of acquiescence, the weekend before the grand dinner, May Kemble DBE appeared on three different Sunday morning television chat-shows; and on the day of the event itself she could be heard on "Good Morning Britain", "The Today Programme" and "The World at One", talking about her early career, the actor-members of Macready's, past and present, and how she had felt when the curtain came down and the men went off to have supper at Macready's without her.

"How dreadful!" said the interviewer.

"Would you believe it, there was a time when women weren't even allowed to *appear* on a London stage?" said Dame May.

"I didn't know that," said the interviewer.

"In Shakespeare's day, the women's parts were played by boys!"

"Before my time."

"We have come a long way since then, and we have a long way to go. But we've had our revenge," added the actress mischievously, in a wonderful gravelly voice. "Before she died, Glynis played Oberon, Hamlet and King Lear."

"Wow! That must have been some production!"

*

Baroness Lovelace gave an interview to 'Makers and Shakers' magazine about the unhealthy menu choices in gentlemen's clubs, and how a long-overdue feminine *touch* would not only be a *breath* of fresh air, but a *taste* of fresh food. She was coy when asked if she would recommend her range of women's dietary supplements to the men of Macready's, mentioning only a few of them and where they could be purchased.

*

Professor Nkosi wrote a three-page article for the Bugle, distributed over the three days leading up to the historic dinner: one page under "Diversity", another under "Equality", and the third under "Inclusivity"; each mercilessly detailing the abominable failings of the handful of gentlemen-only London clubs whose '*hatches remained battened down*' (as she put it) '*against the winds of change*'.

*

The dinner was a ticketed occasion, and very few of 'the forty percent' (who had voted against women membership) applied to take part in what would effectively be a celebration of their defeat. But among 'the sixty percent' (who had voted in favour) were so many desperate to attend, and be *seen* to attend, that places had ultimately to be awarded by ballot. The ballot being truly random, there was no reason why some of the well-known faces of stage and screen who applied for tickets should not have been lucky winners—but, as it happens, every single one of them was lucky. There was less reason, perhaps, why some who had not even entered the ballot should have been lucky winners—but several of those were lucky too.

The pavement outside Macready's was like a budget red carpet at the Oscars. The road had not been closed off, but the gridlocked traffic served just as well. And although much smaller than a Hollywood Reporter press corps, there were enough flashing cameras to allow even the least well-known arrival to convince himself that the moment was all about him.

Patrick 'Roly Poly' Rowlands springs to mind. Isadora Jarre might have let him slip by unnoticed, if he hadn't stood immediately behind a gameshow host she was interviewing and stepped into his place when he left.

"*Macready's has finally come to its senses,*" he said; and wisely anticipating that Isadora would have nothing to ask him, he smiled at the television cameras and moved on, slowly and importantly into the club.

It was never in doubt that Isadora would collar Saul Trencherman. But whatever she had intended as an opening question, the MP cut her off before she had uttered half a dozen words.

"When we last spoke, Isadora, I told you I had joined Macready's with the intention of reforming it from the inside. I am happy to report that my work is done."

"Does that mean that you'll be leaving?" she asked, innocently.

Saul wagged a jocular finger at her—

"Now, now! Naughty!"

Sensing Isadora still had unfired ammunition, Saul manoeuvred his bulk up the steps and away from her, saying over his shoulder—

"Why would I want to leave a club as diverse and inclusive as Macready's?"

The actor-knight whom we met at the club's extraordinary general meeting, and who cannot be named (unless it is above the title) engaged Isadora for an unconscionable time, to her immense frustration, while the great and the good passed by, entering the club without her being able to speak to them.

And what of the three ladies, the stars of the show?

There had been much discussion among them, how to handle their entrance. They were unanimous in deciding that to arrive together would be too contrived. But if separately, in what order? And if one were being interviewed, another could hardly loiter until the interview was over. It was reluctantly agreed that Dame May Kemble, indubitably the most distinguished, had to be the climactic last of them to appear. The second billing went to the first to turn up, a role which Ayana Nkosi grabbed as though she were making a sacrifice. Emily Lovelace had no option but to be the filling in the sandwich.

As things transpired, the gridlocked traffic prevented the ladies' limousines dropping them off at the doors of the club.

So, despite all their planning, they arrived on foot at more or less the same time and were photographed and interviewed as a package deal.

"Oh no!" corrected Dame May Kemble, when a young reporter suggested they '*must be honoured.*' The poor lad was only going to say, '*honoured to be the first ladies elected to Macready's*'. But Dame May was having none of it. "Oh no! Not honoured! Delighted, yes. But not honoured."

"And hold your horses," said Ayana. "We haven't been elected yet."

Emily Lovelace explained: "We are meeting the candidates' committee—"

"Which is how things *usually* go," said Dame May. "There is a procedure, you know."

"And *if* they approve of us," continued Emily, with a rather laboured pause for laughter. Ayanya finished the sentence for her -

"The committee will retire to make their formal decision whether we are suitable to be members of this illustrious club."

"Heaven knows how long that will take them," said Dame May, almost as though she meant it, directing her faux concern to the cameras rather than to Isadora.

The actress led the other two women up the stone steps and into Macready's, to the sound of applause and the lively chatter of newshounds signing-off their broadcasts, and a starburst of flashlights.

*

What the ladies did *not* tell the reporters was that they were heading to a champagne reception in the committee room, at which they were to meet the trustees and a select number of prominent members. The chairman had already confided in them, "*I think we can dispense with the charade of a formal meeting of the candidates' committee, don't you? It would only be for the press, and they won't be there to see it. You have already been elected, after all.*"

When the reception was over, the three ladies would walk down the grand staircase unaccompanied, the doors to the coffee room would be opened at the stroke of eight, and Dame May Kemble would enter, a proud member in her own right, followed by the two other newly-elected ladies (Emily insisted Ayana should go first) and the three of them would be shown to their table before the trustees entered the room to join them.

And what the chairman of the trustees had not told the three ladies, was that when they walked through the doors of the coffee room at eight o'clock sharp, the whole assembly was instructed to rise to its feet and applaud them.

*

As the minute hand of the clock creeps towards the hour, the tension in the coffee room is unbearable. The service of food and drink has been paused, and conversation has sunk towards whispers.

Eight o'clock!

An over-excited member rushes to his feet and makes a fool of himself by clapping enthusiastically before the doors have even opened — or showed the least sign of opening. The doors remain shut, and the premature congratulation sinks back into his chair.

Five past eight!

The whispers revert to the level of normal conversation.

> *Where are they?*
>
> *Making us wait for their big entrance!*
>
> *Actors!*
>
> *Women!*

Ten past eight!

And the conversation sinks back to whispers.

> *Where the hell are they?*

A Quarter past eight!

> *I'd rather like a drink, if that's permitted in my own club?*

Twenty past eight!

The crescendo of restless chatter reaches such a pitch that it can be heard on the pavement outside the club's windows. The thirsty member storms into the kitchen and *demands* that he be served a drink.

Twenty five past eight!

There is a commotion outside the doors to the coffee room.

> *Clunk!*

The sound comes before the doors begin to ease open. The coffee room goes silent.

> *Clunk! Clunk!*

The first crack of space widens between the double doors...

The entire room stands to its feet and a wave of applause and cheering swells to a positive tsunami.

Both doors are flung open...

Bravo!

*I think you mean Brav**a**!*

Oh do shut up!

But not a single national treasure appears. Instead, to the astonishment of the room, Ambrose Harding walks in and stands with his back to the top table, facing the assembly, his face ashen.

What's happened?

What's going on?

Some sit. Others remain standing.

Ambrose waits for the confusion to settle.

"Gentlemen. For reasons which I cannot go into now, this evening's dinner has been postponed."

If Ambrose *did* say any more, it was lost in the cacophony of noise erupting from the coffee room, which could be heard in the street outside and probably halfway across London.

Part Three

1. A letter

While the three national treasures ascended the grand staircase to their champagne reception, a motorcycle messenger in a sinister full-face helmet with a black vizor had pulled up outside Macready's Club and delivered a letter addressed to "The Chairman of the Trustees". It was marked 'Important—Private and Confidential'.

Despite the letter's self-declared importance, the hall porter would not leave his post to take it to the chairman—rightly, with a crowd outside, any one of whom might try to breach the club's defences—and he 'buzzed' for assistance. The deputy arrived and undertook the commission; but seeing the three ladies still on their glorious ascent to membership (which was being filmed), he took the servants' lift to the second floor, where the chairman was in the committee room waiting to receive the fast-tracked candidates—in company with innumerable trustees and celebrities, amongst whom (though it is hardly worth mentioning) the champagne had already begun to flow. The doors of that damnably slow staff elevator opened at the very moment Ambrose Harding's arms opened to greet the illustrious women—"*Ladies! Welcome to your club!*"

The messenger kept a respectful distance from the celebrations and signalled to the secretary to come over, waving the letter at him and mouthing "important". But Pierre (who, if required to choose, would have preferred to witness the elevation of these women to membership of Macready's than witness the ascension of Christ into heaven) shook his angry head and jerked it in the direction of the chairman's office, to which the club servant duly went and left the letter on Ambrose's desk.

There it lay, all the tedious time the ladies did the rounds of the welcoming committee, and one by one the members were presented to their new club-mates.

"Oh, we know each other," said Dame May when confronted with the actor-knight. "He suffocated me in Othello!"

"And you hacked me to death in Agamemnon," laughed the old thespian, as did everyone. The evening could not have been more perfect.

> *And the letter on the chairman's desk didn't jump up and down to draw attention to itself; it didn't send out a warning 'beep', or glow, or sprout legs and run to the chairman and tug at his trousers!*

"I am so happy to meet you," enthused Pierre to Emily Lovelace. "My partner is a devotee—and I have to confess, but don't tell her, I secretly pilfer some of her supplies for myself."

"I can tell," said Emily, enigmatically.

> *Come on, you infernal letter! Can't you see the enormity of what is happening? Do something! Anything!*

But there it lay on the chairman's desk, doing nothing.

Quentin made a beeline for Professor Nkosi.

"Good evening! You probably won't remember me, but I was for the government against you in the Supreme Court. To my eternal relief, we lost. Welcome to Macready's."

"I think you must be mistaking me for someone else. I have never met you in my life, and I have never been in the Supreme Court," said Ayana.

Ambrose Harding chose that unfortunate moment to slip away to the restroom. He passed the open door of his office, where a shaft of late-afternoon summer sunlight had found a direct path through the tall buildings opposite and fallen on the envelope sitting in the centre of his desk, as much as to say "*Look at this!*".

But Ambrose was more taken by the word "Gentlemen" on the door of his destination than interested in what was lying on his desk; and he amused himself with the speculation that Quentin's opinion could mean the word did not need to be changed when the facilities became unisex.

On his return he looked at his watch—7:45. The time had come to present the ladies with their official proclamations of election, which had been specially written in 'court hand' on vellum and placed into red leather folders sealed with the club's coat of arms, as though they were letters patent. They were in a locked drawer on his desk.

And there was the envelope, impossible to be ignored any longer, the shaft of setting sunlight sliding across it, slowly but perceptibly, almost as though it were the letter that was moving and was offering itself to Ambrose. He could not help but see the words "Important, Private and Confidential"; and more out of curiosity than in alarm he casually slit open the envelope with the Graf von Faber-Castel letter opener which had been presented to him by the club on his tenth year as chairman.

He pulled out a single sheet of paper.

*

"You may prefer to leave by the back exit," said Ambrose. "I can arrange taxis, cars, whatever you would like."

"I will leave the way I came in," said Dame May, angrily. She stormed down the staircase in such a fury and in such an uncontrolled passion that she almost missed her footing and fell. Professor Nkosi was close behind, careering down the stairs every bit as livid and hell-bent on shaking the dust of Macready's Club off her shoes as quickly as possible.

Emily Lovelace had a miscellany of clutter to collect — coat, bag, umbrella — so she was nowhere to be seen when May and Ayana bustled out of the building. At that very moment, there came a loud roar from the coffee room. Isadora Jarre was by the roadside, speaking to her cameraman, when the noise awakened the attention of the whole street.

"What's happened, Dame May?"

The actress ignored her.

"Why are you leaving?"

"Is there any reason why I shouldn't?" she snapped back, brushing past her.

Cameras flashed.

Ayana Nkosi clambered awkwardly down the stone steps, heels clicking, and took the opposite direction along the pavement from that which Dame May had charged in search of a taxi. Some insolent reporter yelled after her "Have you resigned?" The call was taken up gleefully by others, delighted not to have missed this unexpected scoop.

"Have you resigned, Ayana?"

"So soon?"

"Have the men behaved inappropriately?"

When she arrived, Baroness Lovelace had arranged the various baggage she was carrying so that it did not look as absurdly inelegant as it did when she left. Umbrella the wrong way up. One loop only of the bag around her forearm, the other dangling, the contents of the bag perilously near to falling out. She had worn her sleek velvet coat on the way in: it was draped over her umbrella-arm on the way out, the belt dragging on the ground.

"What has happened, Emily?" asked an over-familiar Isadora.

"I have no comment," replied the baroness, stiffly.

*

The answer to all their questions, whether they were from the members in the coffee room or the reporters in the street, was to be found on the sheet of paper lying on Ambrose Harding's desk. It was a letter from an old schoolfriend, now senior partner of a 'magic circle' firm of solicitors. It was hand-written, and to that extent informal, but obviously composed in great haste and in language sometimes so guarded that Ambrose was surprised the signature itself was not qualified. The letter said—

> Dear Ambrose,
>
> As you may or may not be aware, my firm is one of the executors of the late Hector Floodgate's will. I am not at liberty to say who the other executors are, suffice it that they know and do not disapprove of my writing this.

To the point—having been made aware of tonight's occasion at Macready's Club (there was a news-item on television), I thought I should write to you, informally, and send it by courier before you receive formal notification in the post—and God knows when that would be these days.

As soon as I was sure it was not professionally improper for me to do so, which I must emphasise I am satisfied it is not, and my co-executors agree, I wanted to let you know that the Hon. Mr. Hector Floodgate has bequeathed his entire estate to Macready's Club and its members—provided membership of the club *"remains restricted to gentlemen only"*.

2. Another problem

It was never going to be easy, how to break it to three formidable 'national treasures' that their triumphant assault on Macready's male chauvinist piggery had been rescheduled, at the very climax of their victory—by a bunch of old men!

But rescheduled it had to be.

The problem, as JJ explained as calmly as he could to a shell-shocked splinter of the house committee, was the word "*remains*" in Hector's will. The bequest to Macready's Club was contingent on membership *remaining* restricted to gentlemen only. And if the club went ahead with the proposal to elect the three women, membership would self-evidently cease to *remain* restricted to gentlemen. And the club would forfeit the bequest.

"Irrecoverably," said JJ.

"How much are we talking about?" asked Saul Trencherman.

"I have heard, it's only gossip mind you, but it may be in the region of two hundred."

"Thousand?"

"Million"

"*TWO HUNDRED MILLION POUNDS?*"

"*Shhhhhhh!!!*"

"That's more than you earn in a week, Quentin," said silk and rayon ruefully.

The sound of three champagne corks popping, one after the other in the committee room, was followed by "*hip, hip, hoorah!*" three times.

"Look out!" said Pierre. The actor-knight had detached himself from the celebrants and was drifting unsteadily towards the open doorway of Ambrose's office.

"I prithee, gentle Ambrose, where are the boys' toilets?"

Ambrose quickly put his arm around the actor and steered him away from his office door.

"My dear fellow. Down here and on the right. Let me show you."

Ambrose all but dragged him along the corridor. The actor peered back over his shoulder at the huddled mass of guilty faces staring at him.

"Been caught smoking in the chemistry lab, have we?"

"Ha, Ha. That's right. Ha, Ha!"

The old thespian found the door he was looking for, and before he disappeared through it, declaimed loudly -

"*And some that smile have in their hearts, I fear, millions of mischiefs.*"

Ambrose returned and shut his office door behind him, muffling the sound of someone making a speech in the committee room.

"We can't possibly proceed with this farcical pageant tonight," said the general.

"It's become a farce, has it?" said Pierre, pouting somewhat.

(Loud applause from the committee room.)

"It has now," said the general.

"I hope everyone understands that we would kiss goodbye to two hundred million pounds if we took *just one more step* towards formalising their membership," said JJ.

"It's amazing how two hundred million pounds concentrates the mind," said the general.

"We can't just ignore two hundred million fucking pounds, general. However distasteful that may be to your sensibilities." Saul had been no stranger to the champagne and struggled a little with the word 'sensibilities'.

Ambrose said the turn of events couldn't be more serious and had to be given careful—and sober—consideration. He proposed they say and do nothing right now, and meet again, with clear heads, early the next morning.

"But what do we tell the ladies *tonight*?" asked Quentin.

(Another loud cheer from the committee room.)

The door to Ambrose's office opened and the actor-knight popped his head round it.

"Chop chop, boys! Curtain up! The audience is getting restless."

His head popped out as incongruously as it had popped in. Ambrose shut the door and locked it.

"We tell them the truth."

"Impossible. What if this letter of yours turns out to be a hoax? It would be better that no one ever knew about it."

"Even if it's genuine, the will could be challenged. Then where would we be?"

"*Can* it be challenged?"

"Yes," said the judge and smooth silk in unison.

"If we don't play this right," said Saul, "we could end up with the worst of all worlds. No bloody money and the whole of London pissing themselves with laughter at us. I need a drink."

"It is absolutely crucial," said JJ, "that we do nothing and say nothing until we know a great deal more than we do now."

"So what do we say to the ladies? Sorry to keep asking."

"I can tell them there is an infinitely regrettable, but unavoidable procedural snag which no-one had predicted, and which prevents us going ahead with the ceremony tonight," said Ambrose.

"It's rather feeble."

"Got any better ideas?"

"Another lie then," said the general.

"There is a great deal at stake!" said Ambrose.

"You don't say."

"I cannot emphasise too strongly," said JJ, "that we say nothing about this, to the ladies, to the members, or to anyone else—until we know exactly how we stand."

"Agreed,"

"Agreed"

"Agreed"

"I will apologise profusely" said Ambrose, "and explain that it really is out of our hands."

We have seen how well his apology went down with the three national treasures.

*

In spite of their promised observance of confidentiality, it was less than an hour before a 'news flash' appeared on the front page of the Bugle Online, under a blown-up photograph of Dame May Kemble storming down the club's steps:

> **Macready's Club is offered a quarter-billion pound bribe to keep its doors closed to women.**
>
> **In an astonishing about-turn, Macready's Club looks set to accept an obscene sum of slave-trader money from a known misogynist rather than admit women as members.**

The mid-day editions carried a cartoon of a judge in a full-bottomed wig sitting on a pile of gold coins, holding his outstretched hand to ward-off the approach of a young female barrister. The caption wrote itself:

Magreedy's Club

3. Another solution

The house committee held an emergency meeting the next morning.

"Who the hell is leaking this stuff?" said Saul. "I can't take a piss without the Bugle reporting it."

JJ fixed his laser eyes on Quentin, like some Marvel Comic villain with super-powers—or one of those sci-fi aliens who any minute might peel off its human mask and reveal a lizard with a forked tongue flicking in and out of its mouth.

Quentin shook his head nervously at JJ—"not me" it said.

Denials came thick and fast—

"Not me," said silk and rayon.

"Obviously not me," said Ambrose.

"Nor I," said Pierre, keen to demonstrate his command of English grammar, and sounding all the more foreign for his pains.

"It could have been anyone," said the general. "The other executors. Someone in the solicitors' office. Anyone. Was the letter unopened when you received it?"

Ambrose nodded.

"It is fruitless to concern ourselves with *who* it was that leaked it," said JJ. "The fact is, it is now in the public domain."

Ambrose told the meeting he had telephoned his old schoolfriend and satisfied himself that the letter was genuine. He had also obtained a copy of the will.

"So, gentlemen. What do we do?"

"It isn't for us to decide," said JJ. "We have no authority. The bequest is to Macready's Club *and its members*. We have no choice but to call another EGM, and let *the members* decide."

"Dear God!" said the general. "Another EGM?"

"Decide what, exactly?" asked silk and rayon.

"Whether or not to accept the bequest."

"On Hector's terms?" asked Ambrose.

"Indeed. We can't dictate any others."

"We'll be a laughingstock."

"We are a laughingstock whatever we do."

"'*I leave two hundred million pounds to Macready's Club and its members*'" said Quentin, cocking his head to one side quizzically. "I wonder what the members will decide?"

"Hasn't this horse already bolted?" said the general, "I distinctly remember a certain EGM at which the majority (not me, I might add) voted that the club's rules do *not* restrict membership to gentlemen. So how can the position *remain* that they restrict membership to gentlemen?"

JJ answered him with the reluctant patience of a schoolmaster explaining something to a dim-witted schoolboy.

"The vote was only to approve the house committee's decision to accept Quentin's advice. It didn't affect *entitlement* to membership, one way or the other."

"Didn't it?" asked silk and rayon.

"Of course not," said the judge irritably. "The rules are the rules: they are not determined by a simple majority vote of members at a general meeting."

"Really?" said Dr. Fleischer. "The impression I gained at the EGM was rather different."

"Don't tell me our members have been misled!" said the general. "Dear me! Whatever next?"

"Surely the problem is my written Opinion," said Quentin. "It was unequivocal. To be blunt, I can't see any way round it."

"There *is* no way, unless we're sitting at the Mad Hatter's tea party," said the general. "Membership of Macready's can't 'remain' restricted to gentlemen, when it's not restricted to gentlemen in the first place."

"Which was what Quentin advised," said silk and rayon. "Wasn't it?"

"In the strongest terms," said Dr. Fleischer.

"And we all accepted your advice, Quentin," said Ambrose. "It is the foundation for this whole sorry business."

Quentin was beginning to wish he'd kept his mouth shut.

"What's more, your Opinion was plastered all over the gutter press," said Saul.

"Courtesy of our resident whistle-blower," said the general.

Quentin took care not to catch JJ's eye, but the gannet had spotted a mackerel struggling against the tide and dived down on him—

"I think it's time you revisit that Opinion of yours, Quentin."

"Revisit it?"

"I really think you should."

"What are you suggesting?"

"That you revisit it."

"Why? I don't think I have ever given such unambiguous, definitive, black and white, incontrovertible advice. Wasn't that the whole point?"

"The whole point?" queried the general, eyebrows raised so high they almost met his hairline.

"Why should I revisit it?" said Quentin, bridling.

The judge shrugged his shoulders. "If you take another look—who knows? You might change your mind."

"On what conceivable grounds could I change my mind, having so publicly slammed the door on any contrary opinion?"

"I really don't know—it's a matter for you and you alone," said the judge, benignly. "But suppose someone drew the Law of Property Act 1925 to your attention. Someone in your chambers, perhaps? Might that give you pause for re-consideration?"

"For God's sake, JJ, don't be absurd! Every first-year law student knows the Law of Property Act 1925."

"I think someone should draw it to your attention nonetheless" persisted JJ, as though Quentin had not, a mere second ago, asserted his and every first-year law student's comprehensive knowledge of it. "It does rather alter things, you see," said the pleasant old judge.

"No. I cannot, I simply cannot, I *will* not, as a matter of professional reputation if nothing else," blustered the now less-than-smooth silk, reddening in the face, "let it be suggested that I need anyone to tell me about the Law of Property Act 1925."

"I think perhaps I should draw it to your attention though," said JJ, with the kindest of smiles.

4. A Difference of Opinion

Quentin's second opinion was short by comparison with his first, because all he needed to do was state the obvious. In his first opinion he had to justify the preposterous.

Brief and to the point though his second opinion was, Quentin's over-use of legal jargon was a barrier to an easy understanding of it—silk and rayon found it particularly heavy going—so Ambrose asked Quentin to provide a reader-friendly summary that could be understood by the layman. This is what Quentin gave him:

> In March this year I was asked for my Opinion on whether the Club's rules permit women to be elected as members of Macready's. My advice was, and is, that in ordinary English usage a masculine word such as "he" in a document means both the masculine and the feminine. The example I gave was the offence of money laundering, where the legislation says that *"a person commits an offence if he acquires criminal property"*. The word "he" must also mean "she". The law would indeed be an ass if the offence of money

laundering could only be committed by a man. The conclusion I reached, therefore, was that the words "he", "him", "man" and even "gentleman" in our Club's rules should be read as including "she", "her", "woman", and "lady".

My attention has since been drawn to section 61 of the Law of Property Act 1925, which introduces an important caveat: a masculine word does not also mean its feminine equivalent if it is obvious from the context in which it is used that it was *intended only to mean the masculine.* A good example may be found in our laws on parental responsibility for children: the word "he" is frequently used in a context which refers it unequivocally to the father, and it is perfectly obvious that it does not mean "she" as well.

I have reconsidered the rules of Macready's Club in light of the Law of Property Act 1925. Having regard to the context in which the rules were drafted and have been interpreted ever since, I am driven to the conclusion that the use of masculine words such as "he", "him", "man" and "gentlemen" in the rules should not be taken as including their feminine counterparts. The words mean no more and no less than what we understand them to mean in everyday usage, and we should not try to squeeze out of them a meaning they were never intended to have.

I am reminded of an extraordinary general meeting of the Club in 1992, at which it was proposed *to amend* the rules of the Club so that *in future* the use of masculine words should always be taken as including the feminine. The proposal was defeated. It would be difficult to find a more compelling context for the purposes of applying the caveat given by the Law of Property Act 1925. At that meeting in 1992, the Club decided by an overwhelming majority that in our rules, "he" does not mean "she"; that "him" does not mean "her"; that "man" does not mean "woman"; and that "gentleman" does not mean "lady".

It follows as night follows day, that our rules do not permit the election of women as members.

*

"And that's the reader-friendly version?" asked the general.
"It is," said Purdey.
"Isn't it what we've been saying all along?" said Martin.
"It is," said Purdey.
"It's utterly shameless," said the general.
"Indeed it is," said Purdey.

5. Another extraordinary general meeting

It would be tiresome to describe what took place outside the theatre, because it followed much the same pattern as before. The press was there in force. Isadora Jarre accosted the great, the good and the not so good. Roly Poly elbowed his way into an interview. The public gaped at the famous faces.

Inside the theatre, however, things were rather different. Everyone who had previously spoken against membership of Macready's being restricted to 'gentlemen' was now in favour. And those who had spoken in favour were now against.

Lord Justice Justice kicked off the speeches.

> "Have you ever tossed a coin to help you decide what to do? If it comes down heads you will do such and such. If it comes down tails, you won't."

The general turned to Purdey in astonishment. "Isn't that what he said last time?"

"Word for word."

"Is he for or against women members?"

"Against."

"What was he last time."

"For."

"And he's using the same speech?"

"The same *beginning*, and I suspect it will be the same *ending*. But I think the middle might change."

And Purdey was quite right -

> "Quentin Latimer KC, than whom no one is more eminent or respected, has interpreted our rules as requiring us, for the present, to put to one side the incontestable equality of women; as requiring us, for the present, to subjugate *to the rule of law* Macready's

commitment to the enlightened principles of merit, fairness, and progress. The rule of law, gentlemen. Above which stands no man. Quentin has advised us, in the highest traditions of self-disciplined analysis, that no matter how much we would prefer to swim with the tide of public opinion; that no matter how much easier it would be for us to escape the calumny of the gutter press; that no matter how dearly we would prefer to welcome, rather than spurn, an untapped pool of talent, expertise and fresh perspectives—qualities in women that would indubitably make Macready's Club a stronger, more vibrant meeting of minds—we cannot do so, because our rules, *the laws of the club,* gentlemen, do not allow it.

A consequence—but by no means a proper motive, and not for the world would I urge it on you—an unlooked for consequence, gentlemen, of accepting Quentin's advice, would be that the club immediately received a bequest of two hundred million pounds.

Do you really want to reject Quentin's disinterested interpretation of our rules? If the coin fell that way, *would you wish it hadn't?"*

There was a moment of total silence—then the dam burst, and an explosion of laughter rocked the auditorium. Some cried helplessly with laughter. Others choked and spluttered with laughter, their neighbours slapping them hard on their backs. JJ waived his hands at them. "No! No!" he said. But the laughter was unabated. They mopped their eyes with handkerchiefs. They drummed their feet on the floor. "Please!" remonstrated JJ. But it would not stop. He turned his back on it, shaking his head in pretend disapproval, and resumed his seat.

The torrent subsided, leaving Purdey to speak next. The theme of his unpromising plea to the decency of members was that although he believed the decision taken at the previous EGM was egregiously wrong, it would be contemptible to reverse it in return for payment. He would have liked Macready's to be a gentlemen's club because it was entitled to be, not because it had been bribed. He urged the club, as a matter of honour, not to accept a bequest on such terms as Hector had stipulated. He received a lukewarm reception.

Our actor knight, once he had done talking about his long association with Dame May Kemble and how deeply and personally he regretted that she could not, after all, join him in membership of Macready's, spoke of all the good that the club could do with Hector's money. Scholarships, subsidies to provincial theatres, "*and some little distribution to each of us, I believe?*" There was a huge cheer from the members.

Then came the general. There was no need, this time, for Pierre to pull the plug on his microphone: the jeering and slow handclapping drowned-out every one of his angry words.

Saul Trencherman MP was the model of righteousness. "Just as our proud nation has laws," he said, "so our fine club has rules. However much we would *like* to admit women as members, and I yield to no one in that ardent desire, we cannot do what the rules do not allow. It's a matter of principle."

Loud shouts of "hear, hear!" and "quite right!" and "what a fine fellow!"

Someone in the audience yelled out—

> *Principle? I thought you said you'd resign if women weren't allowed to be members?*

The MP bellowed "*When the facts change, I change my mind!*"

He received an extended round of applause. But the next day's cartoon in the Bugle was not so kind:

A matter of principle

Hans Fleischer then came to the edge of the orchestra pit and endeared himself to the audience with a psychological analysis of them. "*In denial*" and "*bi-polar legal advice*" were not particularly well received; but it was "*blinded by greed*" that did it for the good doctor. In times gone by, the members would have lynched him.

"I think the mood of the room is clear," said Ambrose when the speeches were over. "But we had better put the motion to the vote. All those in favour of accepting Quentin's revised opinion, please press the 'yes' button now."

The vote was 74% in favour.
Someone yelled -

"*When do we get our money?*"

Ambrose waited for the "*whoops*" and "*cheers*" and "*ker-ching*" noises to die down.

"There will, of course, be a distribution..."

Thunderous applause and '*Hurrahs*'. Different groups, out of sync with each other, sang "*For he's a jolly good fellow.*"

"All in good time, gentlemen! It won't, of course, be the entire sum divided equally among us..."

Shame!

"But I can assure you, it will be substantial."

The singing broke out again. Louder still and louder.

JJ walked to the front of the stage, microphone in hand, and waited patiently for the party spirit to run its course; nodding his acquiescence and smiling at select audience members, pointing his finger at them the way American presidents do.

"The second, and only other motion..." JJ began, but his words were lost in the singing and cheering.

"The second, and only other motion..." he tried again, shaking his head pleasantly at their enthusiasm.

One final attempt—"The second, and only other motion is a proposed rule-change."

A rule change?

"Shhhh!" spread over the stalls seats like steam from a kettle.

"As you know, a rule-change requires a two-thirds majority."

You don't say!

(Huge laughter.)

Can we vote now?

"We have been through a turbulent time, gentlemen, and no one would want us to go through it again. History has shown us that opinions may legitimately differ—"

Even when they're written by the same person!

JJ had to wait for several seconds before the hoots and guffaws died down.

"Opinions may legitimately differ, gentlemen. So, isn't it a prudent course to put things beyond the reach of future differing opinion?"

"A thousand times yes!" cried the actor knight.

"Let me be blunt. Quentin's carefully re-considered advice puts the matter beyond any immediate question. Our rules do not permit women to be elected as members."

Of course they don't.

We all know that.

We've always known that!

"But to guarantee the future, and to make assurance doubly sure..."

"Oh dear! The Scottish play!!" said Roly Poly. "Oh dear!"

"... the proposal before you is to amend the rules by adding **Rule 19 A**; which, subject to your approval, would read: *"For the avoidance of doubt, in construing these rules the masculine does not include the feminine."* In other words, when our rules say 'gentlemen', they mean 'gentlemen'. Strange as it may seem, 'gentlemen' does not mean 'ladies'. Do I hear a seconder?"

A '*seconder*', a '*thirder,*' a '*fourther*', and numbers beyond reckoning shouted their fervent support.

The amendment was approved. The rules were now unambiguous, crystal clear, and rock-solidly invulnerable to different interpretations. Membership of Macready's Club was, and had always been, restricted to gentlemen. The members, skilfully ridden by JJ, had jumped the first hurdle in the Hector Floodgate Stakes, (prize money estimated at two hundred million pounds).

"Oh dear," said Roly Poly as he joined the crush of jubilant members pouring out of the theatre. "I do wish he hadn't quoted the Scottish play."

6. Tactical manoeuvres

Set against the frenzied rage into which Brigit van der Linden flew when she read about the club's *volte face*, Rumpelstiltskin may be thought to have taken his own reversal of fortune rather well. Admittedly, she neither tore herself in half nor stamped herself into the ground, but it took her the whole afternoon and the best part of the next day to clear the broken crockery, replace the shattered mirror, vacuum the goose feathers, and wipe the food and coffee stains from the walls of her little flat in Holborn. The self-inflicted abrasions on her scalp were invisible after a week.

When she was calm enough to type—but it was still with shaking hands—she entered an online 'caveat' at the Probate Registry. This was an ultra-precautionary measure to prevent the executors of Hector's will from obtaining an expedited grant of probate and distributing his estate.

Next, she turned to an artificial intelligence programme on her laptop to get help in the composition of a difficult letter she had in mind writing to Hector's brother, Viscount Floodgate. The programme in question was an 'App' that she sometimes used to help her write opinion pieces for the press.

Artificial intelligence ("AI") is an invaluable tool for those deficient in the natural commodity, and the legal profession is no stranger to its benefits. All a lawyer struggling to achieve a satisfactory 'work/life balance' has to do is upload all relevant source material into the AI programme and let it take over. AI will summarise the principal issues, find inconsistencies, write an advice—whatever you ask it.

"*Certainly, Hal. I can do that.*" is the 2024 computer's response.

But AI is not infallible: much depends on the quality of the material uploaded into it. Brigit had once asked her programme to produce a template email which she could use as a basis for encouraging people she had never met to embark upon litigation. She uploaded several alternative scenarios in which she might want to try to drum up a brief. This is what AI gave her—

> Dear [name]
>
> Please forgive a total stranger writing to you. Be assured that I am only reaching out in case no one else has informed you of your rights.
>
> I was saddened / shocked / appalled / disgusted / intrigued / amused / by the news that you / your partner / mother / father / son / daughter / sibling / dog / have been injured / insulted / mentally abused / deprived of sunlight / arrested / found guilty / dismissed / euthanised.
>
> Please accept my deepest sympathy / condolences / commitment to assist you in any way I can. / I am outraged on your behalf / I am concerned that a great injustice may have been done / I am concerned that a great injustice is about to be done.
>
> There is a groundswell of public opinion in support / despite public opprobrium you should challenge the restraining order / your neighbour should cut down the tree / you have every right to use the ladies' toilets / you should take your dismissal to the Employment Tribunal / I am confident that it is in breach of the Animal Welfare Act 2006.

Are you legally aided? / Have you considered crowd-funding? I can set that up for you.

If I can be of any assistance, on a 'no-win-no-fee' basis, do not hesitate to get in touch.

Brigit thought it possible that, even appropriately adjusted, the template might not set the right tone in the current circumstances. And she had no experience of writing a letter to a peer of the realm. So she uploaded the following request into her AI programme—

> The Hon. Hector Floodgate has died and left his entire estate (worth about 200 million pounds) to Macready's Club, on the proviso that membership of the club remains restricted to gentlemen. I want to write to Hector's brother, Viscount Floodgate—who I do not know and have never met—apologising for writing to him as a stranger, saying how much I sympathise with his loss, etc., sending him my condolences (blah blah blah), and (<u>this is the purpose of the letter</u>) telling him as tactfully as possible, that Hector's will is potentially invalid because (a) it may be that Hector had not the mental capacity at the relevant time to make a will, and (b) the proviso is possibly unlawful on public policy grounds. If Hector's will is invalid, the 200 million pounds will pass to Hector's next of kin—who I understand to be Viscount Floodgate.

In less than ten seconds, her AI programme offered her the following—

Dear Viscount Floodgate,

I hope you will forgive the intrusion of a stranger at this difficult time. Please allow me to express my deepest condolences on the passing of your brother, the Honourable Hector Floodgate. His loss must be a great sorrow to you and your family.

While I hesitate to broach such matters during your period of mourning, I feel compelled to bring to your attention certain legal concerns regarding your late brother's will. I do so with the utmost respect for your brother's memory and your family's privacy.

It has come to my attention that the Hon. Hector Floodgate left his entire estate, valued at 200 million pounds, to Macready's Club, with the proviso that membership remain restricted to gentlemen only. While I have no doubt that your brother's intentions were well-meant, there are two potential issues that may affect the validity of his bequest:

1. There may be questions regarding your brother's testamentary capacity at the time the will was made.

2. The stipulation regarding membership restrictions may be unlawful.

Should these concerns prove valid, it is possible that the will may be declared void. In such a case, the estate would likely pass to your brother's next of kin.

I share this information solely out of a sense of duty and with no personal interest in the matter. I believe it prudent that you be aware of these potential issues so that you may seek appropriate legal counsel if you deem it necessary.

Once again, please accept my sincere condolences for your loss. I apologise for any distress this letter may cause during this difficult time.

Yours sincerely,

[Your Name]

*

Brigit was not alone in seeing potential problems with Hector's will. Quentin and JJ had serious concerns that if a challenge were mounted, there was a real possibility that a chancery judge would declare the will a nullity.

They took a quiet side table in Macready's coffee room to discuss their options.

"It is undoubtedly *vulnerable* (I put it no higher) to the rule against perpetuities," said Quentin.

He was referring to the fact that the wording "*provided that membership of the club remains restricted to gentlemen only*" purported to control the bequest for an indefinite period, potentially for all time. Which, for a reason best known to itself, the law does not allow.

"And we also have the irritating little problem of two conflicting legal opinions written by the same fashionable KC," said JJ — rather unfairly, since he had commissioned both of them. "What's more, my fellow benchers in Lincoln's Inn delight in telling me that the bequest may be contrary to public policy."

Quentin looked wistfully at the centre table where some of those eminent men were dining. "Our only hope is to discuss it with so many of them they have to recuse themselves, until there are no judges left to hear the case."

"Our only hope, my dear Quentin, is to make sure no one challenges the will."

*

Viscount Floodgate was profoundly moved when he read the letter from the trustees of Macready's Club, informing him that they would like, if he gave his blessing, to rename the library "The Hector Floodgate Library". He gladly accepted their invitation to dine at the club and see for himself the very room and its valuable collections of books, paintings and artefacts.

"Which your brother's generous bequest will secure for generations to come," said Pierre.

"He loved Macready's," said the viscount.

"I know," said JJ, "and was much loved in return."

When they had ushered the grateful viscount off the premises, with many an emotional handshake having to be forcibly disengaged, the rascals gathered in the back bar for a stiff drink.

"I think we've done it," said Saul. "Not a whisper of challenge."

"Far from it. He's totally hooked," said Quentin.

"Hook, line and sinker."

"I thought he was going to break down,' said silk and rayon.

'The Hector Floodgate Library. Sticks in the craw a bit," said Saul. "Do we have to go ahead with it?"

"Only until probate," said JJ.

7. Requiescat in Pacem

Hector's funeral was as sad and sombre an affair as the funerals of those who die young usually are. Thankfully, there were no parents to outlive their child and stare in tearful disbelief at the flower-bedecked coffin; but the sight of an older brother and younger sister trying to hide their grief in public but not managing all that well, would have touched the hardest of hearts.

Purdey asked, and was allowed, to say a few words, the poignancy of which only a handful present would have appreciated. It was a conscious variation on the theme of Hector's eulogy for Macready's Club.

> **I first met Hector when he was just twenty one years of age and taken to Macready's Club by his godfather. I liked him immediately, as did everyone, and I was happy to see him elected a few years later. I remember how proud he was to return the honour and invite his godfather to dine with him as his first guest.**

Hector's godfather was in the congregation and lowered his head onto his chest.

> **Macready's was a very special place for Hector. "A refuge", he would say. "A haven". My heart is too full at his passing for me to continue without embarrassing myself.**
>
> **All I will say is 'Goodbye, dear friend. May you rest in peace'.**

*

Hector had been a popular member, and the club was well represented at his funeral, even though it was held in the chapel to Floodgate Hall in North Yorkshire. Some took the train back to Kings Cross. Others stayed with friends who were within driving distance. Purdey, the general and Martin booked overnight accommodation at The Floodgate Arms in the village.

They were in the bar when Viscount Floodgate made a diffident appearance and asked if he could join them for a moment.

"Do forgive my intrusion, Purdey, but I hoped I might find you here."

A chorus of "*of course*", "*can I get you anything?*", "*would you rather speak to him alone?*" was quietly ignored.

"It is awful of me, but I rather think I am about to ask for some free legal advice."

"Fire away."

"I have received this."

The viscount produced a folded piece of paper. It was Brigit's letter. Purdey took it and read it.

"What a truly dreadful woman!" He signalled his passing it to the general.

"May I?"

"By all means."

The general took it, read it, and handed it to Martin.

"Unspeakable!"

"Is she right?" asked Floodgate. "Is it possible the will is invalid?"

Purdey took a long breath and said—

"The bequest to the club is seriously flawed, I can say that much. And if the will were to be challenged … "

Here, he paused and looked intently at Hector's brother.

"...I think a court could *possibly* declare it a nullity. Hector's estate would then pass to his next of kin."

"Thank you," said Floodgate. "I suspected that might be the case. I am so sorry to have broken into your evening and troubled you with this wearisome business."

He turned to go. Then turned back again.

"To clear the air, I have no intention of challenging the will. I want, more than anything, to honour my dear brother's wishes."

"Of course," said Purdey. "I understand."—Which he did.

"What are you going to say to the ghastly Brigit?" asked the general.

"Are you going to bother to reply?" asked Martin.

"I think I have to."

"She hasn't a hope of successfully challenging the will on her own," said Purdey.

"Why not?"

"She's a complete outsider. She stands neither to gain nor lose, whether the will is valid or flawed. The court won't be interested. Her challenge will be struck out."

"Good," said Floodgate.

"She will be livid that you're not helping her," said the general.

"Even better," said Martin.

"What should I tell her?"

"What would your brother have told her?"

"He'd have wanted to make her even more livid."

"Then do that," said Martin.

Floodgate's eyes lighted up, and for a fleeting second the resemblance to Hector was astonishing.

"What would make her *really* angry, d'you think?"

"Insouciant entitlement," said Martin. "Resist putting the witch in her place—be disgustingly pleasant."

Later that night, Viscount Floodgate penned his reply. The diversion gave him a strange relief from the day's awfulness. And the writing left no doubt he and Hector were of the same stock:

> *Dear Brigit (if I may?),*
>
> *Thank you so much for your letter, and for 'tipping me the legal wink'.*
>
> *Your concern for my financial position is touching and much appreciated. Happily, however, we managed to scrape through last year, and my expenses for <u>this</u> year are so enormous that, frankly speaking, Hector's few millions wouldn't make that much of a difference.*
>
> *So my dear, whether my brother's will is valid or not worth the paper it was written on, isn't all that high on my list of priorities.*
>
> *Warmest regards, and good luck with all the fascinating projects of yours that I keep reading about.*
>
> *Vivien.*

He smiled when it was finished, and he placed it in an envelope embossed with the Floodgate crest. Then he broke down in tears. For Hector had come to life while he was writing. And in sealing the envelope he had buried him all over again.

Part Four

1. Challenging Times

The weeks before probate was granted were as enervating for Macready's members as they usually are for beneficiaries to a will, who '*simply cannot understand why it's taking so long.*' But for JJ and Quentin, who knew that it was a distinct possibility the will would not survive a legal challenge, the period of uncertainty was unbearable.

The biggest single threat was a change of heart by Viscount Floodgate. Brigit's 'caveat' was nothing to worry about: she had no legal standing to contest the will, and if she were foolish enough to pursue her challenge, she would face a substantial costs order against her. Viscount Floodgate was another matter. He was the next of kin, and if the will *were* declared void, he stood to inherit another vast fortune.

They invited him to dine at Macready's a couple more times to show him bogus architect's drawings of 'The Hector Floodgate Library', and they were tolerably confident of his being on side. But the violent attacks mounted against the viscount, by Isadora Jarre in the Bugle and by Brigit van der Linden on her Twitter account, put the unholy duo in a permanent state of near-nervous-breakdown anxiety that he might be provoked into changing his mind.

Brigit had been more stung by the cheerful reply signed 'Vivien' than even Martin had wished. She took the light-hearted 'couldn't care less' tone of the letter as the put-down it was intended to be, then she gave it sub-texts undreamed of by its author. To her, his reply was as deliberately insulting as if it had spelled out in block capitals all the offensive, unkind, cruel, inflammatory, playground, classroom, locker room, robing room taunts that she had been the target of (or earnestly believed she had been), ever since she could remember encountering her first toddler in blue baby-clothes.

She began her revenge by leaking her recent correspondence with the viscount to Isadora Jarre, who unfortunately speed-read it and picked up the wrong end of the stick (if not the wrong stick) and wrote a spirited piece for the Bugle in praise of him—

Aristocrat distances himself from slave-money

Macready's Club may have no compunction in being funded by money earned from the slave trade, but the 7th Viscount Floodgate has finer instincts. He refuses to challenge a bizarre bequest, of doubtful legality, make by his late brother the Hon. Hector Floodgate in favour of Macready's Club, because of the connection between his brother's fortune and the slave trade. A source close to the family says that even though the viscount would be the beneficiary of a successful legal challenge, he does not wish to "sully his hands" with the receipt of such a vile inheritance.

Hector's executors wrote a furious letter to the newspaper, stating that his wealth was inherited from his American mother, whose grandfather had laid the foundations by the sweat of his brow, and whose family thereafter had nursed the capital to an immense fortune by good honest work.

The Bugle's apology and publication of the executors' letter prompted a response in faux support from Brigit van der Linden, who innocently pointed out that it was Viscount Floodgate's fortune, not his brother's, that could be traced back to slave-trading.

The paper printed a correction of Isadora Jarre's article, in these terms:

> **The 7th Viscount Floodgate has refused to challenge a bizarre bequest, of doubtful legality, made by his late brother the Hon. Hector Floodgate in favour of Macready's Club. A source close to the family suggests that even though the viscount would be the beneficiary of a successful challenge, he is more than adequately funded by his personal fortune, the foundations of which were laid by his slave-trading ancestor.**

To drive the nail home, Brigit posted a Tweet on her 'X' timeline—

> **It seems that misogyny's blood is coloured blue. Not only did the Hon. Hector Floodgate leave his fortune to Macready's Club on condition it refused to let women be members, but his older brother, Viscount Floodgate, fully supports his women-hating sibling's bequest. Maybe the first Viscount Floodgate only traded in male slaves?**

*

"Shall we get someone to kill her?" asked Quentin... "Joke!"

Nothing in JJ's expression negated the possibility that he took the suggestion seriously.

*

It is not difficult to imagine the trepidation with which JJ and Quentin accepted Viscount Floodgate's surprising invitation to dine with him at Black's, to discuss "*a matter of some sensitivity*".

"What do you think it's about?"

"I have no idea," said JJ. "But I don't like the sound of it."

When they arrived, the viscount gave them a glass of champagne in the bar, but their pleasant pre-dinner chit-chat raised nothing of any 'sensitivity' at all—and neither Hector nor the library project were mentioned.

They proceeded to dinner.

"Before we go in, let me show you something," said Floodgate.

Quentin shrugged his shoulders to JJ behind the viscount's back and made a pantomime of nervously mopping his face with a handkerchief. JJ remained stoney-faced and impassive. They followed Floodgate up the wide staircase.

"This is our library, modest by comparison with what you have planned for Hector's..."

Quentin's hands were behind his back, the fingers on each tightly crossed.

"... but I thought you might like to see these."

He took them to a fine pair of Sheraton bookcases, on which were several handsomely bound volumes of playbills from the eighteenth and nineteenth centuries.

"Black's has had them on loan for goodness knows how long," he said. "I can't think why. They would be much happier in Macready's. I have spoken to the secretary and there will be no difficulty at all in re-housing them when the time comes."

"That is extremely generous," said JJ.

"Hector was very fond of Restoration Comedy," chanced Quentin.

"Really? I didn't know that."

*

The viscount's manner, his talk of 'Hector's' library, the proposed 're- housing' of the volumes of playbills, these were inconsistent with a change of heart, or a *complete* change of heart, at any rate. But nothing that could be called "a matter of some sensitivity" had yet arisen; and although JJ and Quentin were partially relieved, there was a palpable tension across the table while they dined. It was not until they were having coffee afterwards, that Floodgate said—

"The sensitive issue I mentioned in my letter..."

Vivien Floodgate was clearly finding what he was going to say a little embarrassing.

"Oh yes," said Quentin casually. But he was on the edge of his seat.

"You may have seen various things about me written in the Bugle?"

"I have."

"We have."

"Utterly disgraceful."

"Rather unpleasant," said Floodgate. "But it got me thinking."

"Thinking?"

"Have you complained to IPSO?" asked Quentin, not yet having sufficiently steeled himself against the hammer-blow of bad news and hoping to divert the pending disappointment, even if only for a few minutes.

"I have no intention of responding in any way at all. *'Never complain'*, as they say."

"Quite right," said JJ.

"No. I wanted to let you know, having in mind the suggestions that keep appearing in the newspapers that I ought to challenge Hector's will..."

The blood drained from Quentin's face.

"Ahh... yes... that," said JJ, as though nothing had been further from his mind.

"I wanted to let you know, in case you had any doubts..."

"Doubts?"

"My dear fellow!"

"... that I would not dream of doing so, under any circumstances. Aside from its likely to be an ugly business, dirty linen in public and all that, as far as I'm concerned Hector's wishes are paramount. I thought I ought to let you know."

Relieved of his burden, he smiled at them disarmingly. "Would you like anything with your coffee?"

"Brandy please!"

"Yes. Brandy would do it!"

"Ha, Ha. Yes. Brandy! Splendid!"

2. Calm before the storm

Viscount Floodgate could not wish-away the days more quickly in which he waited for probate to be granted and '*the whole sorry business done with.*' The date had at last been set for the hearing of the executors' application for dismissal of Brigit van der Linden's 'caution'. The viscount had been advised that Brigit had no legal standing to contest the will and she was certain to fail. But waiting for her challenge to be struck out, however inevitable that might be, kept him sleepless at night and listless by day.

The weekend before the hearing, he decided to take his mind off "*the law's delays*" and set about the task which he had been avoiding until it simply had to be done: sorting and disposing of Hector's personal effects.

Hector's housekeeper had already cleared the Kynance Mews property of rubbish (and perhaps some gold cufflinks and loose change on his dressing- table); she had emptied the fridge, laundered the linen, boxed-up some ornaments and other free-standing bric-a-brac, and dusted and aired every room.

But decisions about what was to be kept, what was to be given to charity, what was to be sold, what was to be thrown away, these were the dread tasks that most of us have to face, sooner or later, after a death in the family. And Viscount Floodgate decided that the weekend before the court hearing was as good a time as any to face them.

How forlorn the empty house of a dead person is!

Two large cardboard boxes lay immediately the other side of the front door. One had a cushion sitting on top of it, with a toaster, an alarm clock, a glass vase, a child's toy dog, a disconnected telephone, an electric kettle and four silver picture frames placed higgledy-piggledy underneath. The other box had bedlinen and towels still in their cellophane laundry wrappings, crammed inside to the point of over-flowing. The day's circulars and spam mail were scattered on the floor. Older correspondence had been placed on the hall table.

The blinds were drawn throughout the house. The pictures had been taken down and lay against the walls of their host rooms, one beside another, leaving tell-tale signs of picture-hooks and the outlines of their frames behind them.

Books were stacked in a half-dozen boxes in the drawing room. The viscount made a mental note to have the best of them shipped to the Hector Floodgate library in Macready's, when the time came. He wondered how many concerned restoration comedy but left the inspection of them to a later date. A Panama hat was on top of one of the boxes, its band in the Macready colours.

Hector's school cricket bat still hung on his bedroom wall—perhaps because it was not immediately apparent how to dismount it from its fixings without scratching it. The bruised handwriting across its flat surface said—

Today I scored 50 not out against Castlereagh House

*

It was not easy, at first, for the viscount's moistening eyes to read the loose mail on the hall table. The unpaid utilities bills should not have led to such hasty court-summonses—but one of them had, and he put it in his inside coat pocket to hand to the executors for immediate attention.

There was a wedding invitation, similar to one he had received weeks ago, and instantly recognisable from its return address to be from a cousin in New York, who obviously had not known of Hector's death at the time of posting. She knew now: her touching letter was sitting on Viscount Floodgate's desk in Yorkshire.

The familiar masks of comedy and tragedy caught his eye, embossed on the off-white envelope of one unopened letter. He rightly guessed it was from Macready's Club, and in a momentary release from the misery of his visit he smiled to himself, remembering how Hector loved the club, loved entertaining him there and boasting about the paintings in the coffee room — "*the best dining room in London*" he used to say — rubbing it in how much nicer the room was than '*that VIP lounge*' (as he called it) in Black's.

The viscount slit the envelope and opened the folded letter, which was typed. It was from the club secretary and was as follows —

Dear Mr. Floodgate,

This is to inform you that on 17th April 2023 the House Committee resolved unanimously to expel you from Macready's Club with immediate effect, on the grounds:

1. Despite numerous warnings over a substantial period, you have repeatedly conducted yourself otherwise than as a gentleman.

2. Your gross misconduct has brought Macready's Club into disrepute.

3. On the night of 5th March, when drunk in the coffee room, you shouted profanities at Lord Justice Justice. Given the opportunity to apologise,

you refused to do so in an insolent and offhand manner calculated to offend him further.

I cannot let this letter be committed to the post without adding on a personal note (although I am confident I speak for the Trustees and House Committee) that I will be relieved to see your membership at an end. From the day you were elected, you have been an embarrassment to the Club and its members.

Though you cannot be prevented from returning as a guest, it is hoped that if a member should invite you, you will resist the temptation to accept.

Please make arrangements for the wine which I am told you keep in the club's cellars (though on what authority escapes me) to be removed forthwith, in default of which it will be destroyed.

Pierre Moreau.

*

The trustees of Macready's Club fiercely resisted Viscount Floodgate's late application to take over Brigit van der Linden's challenge to Hector's will. The executors took a neutral stance, and the judge ruled in favour of the viscount. He instructed Purdey to represent him.

"I was going to resign anyway," said Purdey.

*

"I don't understand him," said silk and rayon. "Now he says that our rules *do* allow women to be members. Am I missing something?"

"What Purdey says is that we were on the point of electing three women, so the inference must be that membership of the club had not '*remained*' restricted to gentlemen," said Quentin.

"Is that all?" said Pierre.

Quentin raised his eyebrows to JJ, who didn't respond.

"I can't be doing with him," said Saul. "I think he spends his waking hours looking for a high horse to ride."

"Never liked him," said JJ.

3. Floodgate v The Trustees of the Estate of Hector Floodgate (deceased)

The courtroom was packed. Most of Macready's trustees sat in the public gallery, with JJ ready to stare the judge into submission if he looked at all 'unreliable'. Viscount Floodgate positioned himself as far as he could from JJ and Saul Trencherman, both of whom assiduously avoided eye contact with him. Surprisingly, the club secretary, Pierre Moreau, was nowhere to be seen.

The press was there in force, but Isadora Jarre was not among them: she was in Calais reporting on a 'Boats for Migrants' campaign the Bugle was sponsoring. She gave the task of reporting on London's *trial du Jour* to the paper's sketch-writer, a scholarly-looking man with a mischievous eye, who took to his assignment with relish. His account of the first day of the hearing appeared in the online edition within a couple of hours, and it read—

> **I don't think I have seen such a sea of curly white hair since I looked out over the cotton fields of Texas in my gap-year. The somewhat tattered barristers' wigs on the front row of KCs were supplemented by as many (newer) white wigs of their juniors behind them. And if that were not enough horsehair, we should add the spotless, almost luminous white wigs of their pupils in the row behind *them*. A cartoonist might have drawn thought-bubbles emanating from the heads of the fee-earners, with Lamborghinis, house extensions, yachts and Caribbean holidays filling them. Your sketch-writer wondered if the legal costs might exhaust the entirety of Hector Floodgate's estate;**

but a barristers' clerk told me, with a trembling voice and ill-concealed outrage at the unfairness of it, that the lawyers' fees *'probably wouldn't even amount to a million.'*

Sir Charles Holland KC was first on his feet, and announced on behalf of the executors that they were taking a neutral position. The judge remarked that, having read Sir Charles' neutral skeleton argument, he wouldn't like to have to face him in a case where he took a hostile position. There was laughter in court. Sir Charles explained that his role was merely to assist, and that, of course, the executors would distribute the estate in accordance with his lordship's judgment. *"Is there anything you would like to add to your neutral forensic evisceration of Viscount Floodgate's challenge,"* asked the jovial old judge. Sir Charles shook his head and sat down.

Young James Purdey KC (for Floodgate) sprang to his feet like a gazelle. For the life of me, his junior looked old enough to be his father. His case was simple: either the deceased's will was void because it offended the rule against perpetuities, or the proviso to the bequest had not been met, because membership of the club had self-evidently ceased to be restricted to gentlemen — otherwise three distinguished ladies would hardly have been invited to join.

When Quentin Latimer KC (for Macready's) stood to reply, with the languid air of someone who surely didn't need to, the judge said he needn't trouble him on the 'perpetuities' point, because in his judgment, on a proper interpretation, the bequest required only that membership remained restricted to gentlemen '*up until distribution of the estate*'. It did not tie Macready's to that condition in perpetuity. "*Quite so, my Lord,*" said Latimer. A footballer would have been skidding along on his knees lifting his shirt up and down.

But the match was not over. "*I am more troubled,*" said the judge, *"by the election or near-election of the three ladies. Surely, the inference to be drawn from that occasion is that the club, at some point in time before then, it doesn't matter when, had decided to admit women?'*

Was this a free kick to Purdey? But Latimer showed no sign of concern. There was a flurry of activity on the substitute benches. A solicitor passed a piece of paper to a pupil barrister, who skilfully passed it to his pupil supervisor, who deftly passed it to Quentin Latimer. *"Your Lordship will have seen,"* he said, *"that I have been handed a document. Might I have a moment to read it?"* The judge nodded. The premier league KC read it. Or made a show of reading it. Is it too cynical of your sketch-writer to wonder if he had seen it before?

It turned out to be an affidavit sworn by the secretary of Macready's that very morning, which is why it had not been available until then. Though the ink was not yet dry on the paper, there were copies for the judge and for everyone else, which appeared from nowhere like so many rabbits from a magician's hat.

Latimer was on his feet again in an instant, with arguments so persuasive one might almost have thought he had prepared them in advance of this wholly unexpected development.

"*The affidavit states in clear, unambiguous language, my Lord, that on the night of July 1st, 2023,* *the three ladies left Macready's Club before they were elected. The candidates' committee had not even met. It may well have been hoped that the committee would meet and elect the ladies, but they had not yet done so when the ladies left the club. Unless and until the ladies were actually elected, membership of the club remained restricted to gentlemen. It was open to the candidates' committee to reject their proposals for membership for that very reason. I respectfully submit that no inference should be drawn that the committee's decision would necessarily have been in the ladies' favour. The events of that night surely demonstrate that however likely something may be, likelihood is not the same thing as certainty."*

"*Do you have an application, Mr. Purdey?*" asked the judge. (Which in translation means "You're pretty well screwed, aren't you?") The judge was clearly enjoying the roller-coaster. To your sketch-writer's eyes, young Purdey looked a little shaken. He requested, and was given, an overnight adjournment to consider this compelling new evidence.

HALF TIME SCORE — Macready's 2: Floodgate 0

*

"It's not looking good," said Purdey.

They were in his chambers for a de-brief.

"Anything in particular stand out as the worst blow?" asked Viscount Floodgate.

"The secretary's affidavit is a killer," said Purdey. "I bet Quentin has had it up his sleeve for weeks. He has a reputation for ambush."

"What about your 'perpetuities' argument? You thought that was our best point."

"I still do. But *il judice* obviously doesn't agree. I'm surprised. I think he's wrong. But that's where we are—unless you want to go to the Court of Appeal?"

Floodgate smiled and shook his head. "It would be greedy to ask for the pleasure of all this a second time. So, what do we do?"

"Our perpetuities point having gone up in smoke, the only way we can win is by establishing that on July 1st the three women were actually elected. I thought it was a pretty obvious inference from the facts—but the secretary's affidavit has put a rather large spanner in the works. I'm sorry, Vivien. I really am. I thought we were home and dry."

"They're a clever bunch, aren't they," said Floodgate.

"The majority on the house committee are either KC's or judges," said Purdey.

The buzz of Purdey's mobile phone broke the downbeat atmosphere. He answered it and waived to the others that they needn't leave the room. Then he stood, and with the receiver pressed against his ear, he paced up and down.

"Yes ... Yes ... Of course ... I'll have to take instructions, obviously ... This is all rather sudden, Quentin ... Are you going to tell me why? ... If you must ... As I keep saying, I'll have to take instructions."

He hung up and returned to his seat.

"Well, that's *very* odd. They are asking if we would agree to a 'costs amnesty'."

"What's that?"

Another opportunity for Purdy's junior: "It's an agreement, that whoever wins or loses, each side pays its own costs."

"Why on earth would they offer that, half-way through the case?" asked Floodgate.

"I have no idea," said Purdey.

"It's a sign of weakness," said his junior.

"Hardly, after what happened in court today. More likely it's a bully-boy's taunt, to unnerve us," said Purdey. "But let's take it at face value. It would mean that if we lose, and as things stand that's a rather small 'if', you would not have to pay Quentin Latimer's astronomical fee."

"And if we win?"

"They would not have to pay mine."

"My brother had a coarse expression," said the viscount, "of which I thoroughly disapproved. But it might be appropriate now."

Not for the first time, Vivien Floodgate's wry smile was uncannily like his younger brother's.

"Tell them to '*go fuck themselves in every conceivable way*'."

4. Day Two

The headline read:

> **Dramatic twist in episode two of the Macready soap-opera**

And the rest of the sketch was as follows—

> **The sense of loss was palpable. For a moment I thought I could see, shimmering above their white wigs, the mirages of Lamborghinis and Caribbean holidays dissolving into nothing. I felt most sorry for the juniors, who in the highest traditions had done no work at all and were looking to be handsomely rewarded for their efforts. To paraphrase Mike Batt: "How could their hopes that burned so brightly suddenly burn so pale?"**

At first, the answer was a mystery. To sketch-writers of little brain, such as I, there did not seem anything in the least extraordinary about a witness coming forward to give evidence. Isn't that what usually happens in courts? Were all those episodes of "Judge John Deed" a big lie? Yet, when James Purdey asked for permission to call the chairman of Macready's Club to give evidence, all hell broke loose. Quentin Latimer KC, pale-faced and furious, raised every objection under the sun, moon and stars. One would have thought Purdey was asking permission to strangle a new-born baby. Of course, the smooth silk wrapped it up in coded barristers' language, such as "*My learned friend has perhaps forgotten the usual courtesies*". But you wouldn't need to be Alan Turing to break the code: "*The crooked prick is up to his old tricks again.*"

The judge listened to Latimer patiently, then ruled in favour of Purdey without calling on him to reply.

Ambrose Harding, the aforesaid chairman, as amiable and clubbable an old cove as your sketch-writer could ever wish to take a drink from, then gave evidence on oath. He had been in court when the secretary's affidavit was read to the judge. He was concerned that the facts stated by the secretary were not as he recollected, and when the case was adjourned overnight, he had sought legal advice. Which resulted in his making himself known to James Purdey KC this very morning. He told of a meeting of the candidates' committee on the afternoon of 1st July 2023, at which three distinguished ladies were formally elected as members of Macready's Club. He produced the minutes of that meeting, as well as three leather-bound proclamations, printed on vellum, signed by each of the trustees. Your sketch-writer thought that the archaic wording of the proclamations was rather pretty. James Purdey suggested it was rather conclusive. The opening words of each were similar, the only difference being the name of the new member.

Be it known that on this day in the first year of the reign of King Charles the Third, and in the year of Our Lord 2023, May Kemble DBE was elected to membership of Macready's Club. In witness thereof...

There was no cross-examination. Latimer asked for a short adjournment. In the strange world of lawyers, units of measurement are not the same as they are in the real world. A 'small brief fee' can be tens of thousands, and a 'short adjournment' can last hours. After some 90 nerve-wracking minutes, the barristers returned to their seats. The atmosphere was electric. The judge came back into court and a doleful Quentin Latimer got to his feet and dropped a bombshell -

"As your Lordship will have seen from the terms of the draft Consent Order handed up to your Lordship in chambers a few minutes ago, the parties have reached agreement as to the outcome of this case, subject of course to your Lordship's approval."

For most of us in the room, a bomb had definitely been dropped—but it had not gone off.

It remained unexploded in the well of the court. What on earth was Quentin Latimer talking about? Why can't they speak English? The judge asked if the trustees of Macready's Club now accepted that membership had <u>not</u> 'remained' restricted to gentlemen, which meant that the proviso attaching to Hector Floodgate's bequest to Macready's Club had <u>not</u> been met, and that the deceased's estate should therefore pass to his next of kin, Viscount Floodgate.

"That is now accepted, my Lord," said the despondent KC.

Ker- BANG!

The case had been settled. A lucrative three-to-four-day gravy train had slammed on its brakes after only one stop. There was truth on the line.

Poor barristers! Bye-bye, the Caribbean! Hello, the Norfolk Broads!

5. Shock waves

When the triumphant Team-Floodgate left court, they were set upon by a press corps hungry for soundbites. They got nothing—until an impudent reporter shouted:

"What are you going to do with the money, Lord Floodgate?"

"It's not mine to spend," said Vivien. "It's my brother's."

No one, not even his own team, had the faintest idea what he meant by that. The charitable among them wondered if the viscount was, as they believed most of the hereditary peerage were, slightly off his head.

Purdey waited for an appropriate moment before asking him. They were having dinner in Black's, to celebrate their victory.

"Hector didn't leave it to *me*, you see," explained Vivien.

"But it's yours now, whether you like it or not."

"I understand. But I wouldn't be comfortable keeping it. Simple as that. Forgive my being gross, but I do have rather a lot already. Don't get me wrong: it would be delightful to receive Hector's millions. But that wasn't his plan, was it? "

"Clearly not."

"And I am determined to honour his plan, at least the spirit of it, if I can, without letting Macready's have one penny of his money."

"Do you have anything in mind?"

"I've been asking myself, what would *Hector* do if our roles were reversed."

"And?"

"What do you think of this ... Suppose I used his money to set up another club, as close to a replica of Macready's as possible?"

"Gentlemen only?"

"Do you really have to ask?"

"What a lovely idea! They will be furious."

"Is it something you'd be interested in joining, if I went ahead?"

"Of course I would!"

"Do you think many others would be?"

"They'll be hammering at the door."

"I've found premises," said Vivien, with growing enthusiasm now his idea had Purdey's approval. "A small hotel in Covent Garden. It used to be a rather grand house. I'm told Irving stayed there when he had the Lyceum."

"Perfect!"

"It went out of business in the pandemic. It has everything we could wish for. A large hall. Kitchens, of course. A modest number of bedrooms—some could be turned into offices. And we could knock a few walls down, *et voila!* a billiards room."

"Excellent!"

"And there are cellars, obviously. And it goes without saying, a ballroom—which would make an excellent dining room."

"Macready's coffee room will take some replicating."

"I've thought of that. The National Trust has some paintings of mine on loan, dotted around here and there. I wouldn't have wanted to call them in for no good reason. But the Trust has become so frightfully 'woke' of late, it wouldn't cost me a thought to have them back. What do you think?"

"Beyond excellent!"

"They're not theatrical paintings, I'm afraid. But there's nothing we can do about that. If our members could bear to exchange those brightly coloured portraits of actors making strange gestures for the odd Cezanne or Raphael, I'm sure our coffee room could hold its head up high. What do you think?"

Purdey was immensely flattered that the viscount talked in terms of "*we*" and "*our coffee room*". He was overcome by a sense, not exactly of joy but of sublime content, of a kind he had not felt since he sat with Hector in the gardens of the Wayfarer's Club, listening to a blackbird 'singing in the dead of the night' — the last time he saw Hector alive.

He dared to echo Vivien's familial language -

"What shall we call it?"

"Hector's of course!"

*

Pierre Moreau was summonsed before the judge to answer why he should not be committed for trial for perjury. But he did not appear. He had not been seen since the hearing, and his whereabouts were unknown. A warrant was issued for his arrest, but never executed. There were rumours of sightings now and then, of his running a casino in Macau, a hotel in New Zealand, and (possibly malicious gossip) a brothel in Bangkok.

*

Pierre Moreau not appearing, the judge called everyone on Macready's legal team before him, to answer what part they had played, what they knew or should have known.

Quentin Latimer KC had no idea, of course, that he had been handed a false statement. He took it at face value and assumed its veracity had been checked. The solicitors who produced it had only been given sight of the document that morning and assumed it had been sent to them by the trustees. The trustees had been as surprised as anyone when the document was produced. They knew nothing about it. When it was handed to the judge, they assumed it had come through the solicitors.

"*All these assumptions,*" remarked the judge drily. "*Almost biblical.*"

No one could have been more shocked and appalled by the secretary's lying affidavit than Lord Justice Justice. "I suppose you, too, assumed it was in order," asked the judge. "*I assumed nothing,*" snapped JJ. "*I had no knowledge of it one way or another.*"

Not one of the conspirators, if that's what they were, let another of them down. They formed a tight ring of mutual cooperation, the very opposite of a Roman suicide circle, each man protecting the back of the man on his left rather than killing him, defeating any prospect of the affair ruining anyone's life except Pierre Moreau's.

*

The smell of scandal lingered on. Saul Trencherman MP was advised by the Party chairman to distance himself from Macready's or face losing his seat at the next general election. Accordingly, he resigned. And at the next general election he lost his seat.

After some delay, occasioned by his proximity to events of questionable propriety, but with no evidence at all to suggest he was party to them, JJ was eventually appointed to the Supreme Court. As predicted, his title 'Lord Justice' made it sound to the general mass as if he were still a Court of Appeal judge. To his intense irritation it became a standing joke amongst his peers in the House of Lords that he was still down there in the Strand with the Lord and Lady Justices.

Silk and rayon, striving more mightily for himself, perhaps, than ever he had for a client, was nonetheless unsuccessful in obtaining a 'pension-pot' brief in the Covid Enquiry. He was not even seriously considered. Despondent, he decided to throw in the towel and retire with his wife and dog to a small cottage in the Cotswolds, where not long afterwards he became chairman of the Parish Council; in which capacity he was accorded a gratifying level of respect unfamiliar to him in all his years as a defence silk in the Central Criminal Court.

The Cotswolds not being 150 miles from London, he was ineligible for the reduced 'country membership' subscription to Macready's Club, and he resigned in anger. "*When you think of all I have done for them!*"

*

The club was back where it had been before the reformers' campaign started on its reckless course—but without Hector's millions, with its reputation in tatters, and the millstone of a strict 'gentlemen only' rule hanging round its neck.

It had indeed become the nation's laughingstock. A byword for chicanery and chaos. Resignations were rife. Actors, who had campaigned so hard (and so noisily) to propel the club into the twenty-first century, wouldn't be seen dead in it now it had returned to the twentieth. Even humble civilians who had never graced a stage or read the news on television, whose faces were unknown, and whose opinions had nothing to fear from a cancel culture, even they hesitated before wearing the Macready tie in public.

At the next annual general meeting, everyone on the house committee was unceremoniously thrown out. Not only had they let an inheritance of two hundred million pounds slip through their fingers, but to '*make assurance doubly sure*' they had persuaded an EGM to set in stone what at best had been a questionable rule against women membership.

"I told him he shouldn't have quoted the Scottish play," said Roly Poly Rowlands.

6. Arrivals and Departures

The exodus from Macready's had consequences which no one had predicted, or even contemplated as possible. Many more '*status quo*' members resigned than did '*reformers*', so to everyone's amazement the balance of prejudice slowly tilted back in favour of allowing women to join. The rotating composition of the house committee, coupled with some timely resignations, accelerated its return to the more progressive persuasions of its recent past. And in the blink of an eye, the received wisdom was that the new mix of members might j<u>ust</u>—"*maybe*", "*hopefully*", "*I pray to God we're right*"—be in favour of electing women, even to the extent of a two-thirds majority.

In trepidation, and with no illusions as to the ridicule that would rain down on them, two feckless members were strong-armed into proposing and seconding a motion to change the rules back, again (was it only for the second time?), and the proposal was placed on the Agenda for the *next* AGM. The club bit the bullet and braved the mockery. The motion was put, and more than two thirds voted in favour. Rule 19A was repealed. Masculine words in the club's rules were henceforth to be interpreted as including their feminine counterparts. Women could become members of Macready's Club.

It was pure gold to the press. A cartoon in the Bugle showed the well-known exterior of Macready's Club with two uniformed hall-porters in the open doorway—

If Macready's reputation had not plummeted far enough into the abyss, an insane sub-committee thought it a good idea to re-invite the three national treasures to be the 'first lady members'. Dame May Kemble and Professor Ayana

Nkosi did not dignify the sublimely insensitive invitation with a reply. Baroness Lovelace, however, sent a letter of just four words:

"**You must be joking**".

The unwritten response that Dame May Kemble had been tempted to send comprised just two words.

*

Macready's, however, could not let go of the desire to trumpet its re-discovered devotion to Diversity, Equality and Inclusion. It was determined to have reports of a ceremonial banquet, welcoming the historic election of women to the 150 year-old club, emblazoned on the front pages of every newspaper. The first choice of 'national treasures' having turned their backs on them, the club sent invitations to the second choices: if not national treasures, they were 'much valued do-gooders'. But after what had happened before, the second choices were not prepared to take the risk of a similar humiliation, and the invitations were politely declined. A third tranche of invitations was then sent to some even less well-known, but well-thought-of women 'sportspersons' and 'TV personalities' (daytime). But they got wind of the earlier choices (who had delighted in telling them) and they politely, but this time a little frostily, refused to take the bait.

The club's desperation to find *any* woman prepared to be the celebrated 'first' became the joke of London. Purdey, in an homage to Hector's newspaper appeal for 'safe clubs', posted a half-page spoof on 'X' along similar lines:

URGENT APPEAL

The men of Macready's live in sub-human conditions. They eat barely edible food because *they have no choice*. They never complain. A woman would complain. Just one new woman member a week could see a complaints book filled to overflowing within a year.

Day after day, Macready's Club trawls the streets of London in search of someone to be the first woman member. But women simply do not want to join.

WON'T YOU HELP?

Eventually, the house committee came to terms with the fact that it had become impossible to invite anyone to be the celebrated "first" without insulting them. The grand scheme was dropped. Women were proposed in the ordinary way, their elections were expedited, and the first woman member of Macready's sat down at the centre table without anyone knowing who she was, or realising, least still celebrating, the significance of her attendance.

*

Isadora Jarre had looked forward to her triumphant entrance as a new member, and more still to writing about it in her column. But her pre-prepared piece, with names and anecdotes to be filled-in as appropriate (and invented if necessary), was abandoned in its entirety when she got back to her computer in the Bugle's headquarters in Wapping. She had endured what she later described as '*the most excruciatingly dull evening of my life*', and began her new column with the headline:

Ladies—Why did we bother?

The writing was vintage Isadora, with perhaps the best of it—

I felt like Dorothy in "The Wizard of Oz". It had been a long journey, full of promise, but when I got there all I found was an old man talking gibberish. And you better believe me, there were plenty more like him! The monkeys would have been better company. Oh, for those red slippers!

She never returned to Macready's and never again wrote about it.

*

Brigit van der Linden found a handful of left wing journalist members willing to propose her, and she abandoned her phoney claim that '*wild horses couldn't drag her across the threshold of Macready's Club*'. In fact, she longed to exult in her victory over the club and its male chauvinists. She couldn't wait to sit down unaccompanied at the centre table and '*know more about the rugby than the men did*'. Or stand at the bar upstairs and cause Bateman Cartoon horror by ordering pints of Guinness and 'snake bites'.

The day she received a letter telling her she had been elected, she went out and purchased a Macready tie—the vibrant one. Then she returned to her flat in Red Lion Street and took a 'selfie', wearing the tie around her neck, quite loose but knotted as a tie usually is. She planned to send it the Bugle, upload it onto Facebook, 'X', Snapchat, Instagram,

TikTok, and LinkedIn, and place copies of it in the pigeon-hole of every male member of her proxy chambers.

Her camera sent the picture to her chambers' printer wirelessly, and she walked across to Gray's Inn to collect the printouts, brazenly wearing her new tie *en route*.

It was a large, industrial printer/copier, capable of taking thick cardboard sheets for glossy photographs. She had requested forty seven copies. In colour. As she leaned over to retrieve the first of them, the thin end of her tie rested on the paper tray and was pulled into the guts of the machine. A domestic printer might have jammed, but this one had taken thicker cardboard than the thin silk of the Macready tie and had no intention of jamming. Disney would have anthropomorphised it, giving it two malevolent eyes and the determination of those relentless brooms in "The Sorcerer's Apprentice".

She only noticed what was happening when her head was tugged forward. Instead of simply turning off the printer, she unwisely tried to pull the tie out. The printer had other ideas, and inch by inch it gobbled up more. By the time she gave up battling against the superior force of the industrial machine, her head was only three or four inches above the paper tray.

Too late, she felt for the off-button on the control panel—but whatever it was she pressed, it wasn't "off". She tried loosening the knot which was now hard against her throat—but the taut, thin end of the tie being pulled inexorably into the photocopier made loosening the knot impossible. Her hands flayed around, looking for the scissors she had seen lying close by. They were too far away. The tie tightened round her neck. She called for help. The tie tightened tighter still.

They found her dangling from the photocopier, quite dead, strangled by the Macready tie. The junior clerk remarked, and was severely disciplined, '*It was a shame her head hadn't landed on the glass pane and got photographed like a Christmas party bum-pic.*'

7. Et Lux Perpetua

Viscount Floodgate was as good as his word and impetuous in the execution of it. He secured the freehold of the old hotel, obtained the necessary listed building and planning consents, and exhausted a good slice of Hector's money on lawyers, architects, historians, designers, cabinet makers and upholsterers. After almost a year, and with restoration nearing completion, the fine old building was on course to achieve a magnificence that even in its 19th century heyday it could never have dreamed of.

The day came when Hector's Club was ready to be launched!

Membership was by invitation only: Vivien Floodgate was the sole proprietor, the building was his personal property and he could invite in, or chuck out, whomever he pleased. All the forty percent who had voted against allowing women to be members of Macready's were invited to join. A healthy majority accepted. Of the sixty percent who had voted in favour, many were known to have done so reluctantly, and they too were invited. Disaffected members of Sprats and the Symposium (which had also gone co-ed, not to everyone's satisfaction) made up the numbers.

None of Macready's staff were directly approached (that would have been beyond the pale, said Floodgate) but more than a third made unsolicited applications for employment. Every one of them was offered a position. Some achieved promotion.

Ambrose Harding had resigned from Macready's the night before he gave evidence in the High Court—evidence which we have seen snatch two hundred million pounds away from Macready's outstretched claws. Floodgate offered him chairmanship of Hector's, but the dear fellow declined, saying *'he had had more than enough of that kind of thing for one lifetime'*. He accepted life-membership instead, with engaging modesty.

Purdey drew up the rules. There weren't many — the members whom Floodgate would invite were expected to know how to behave. Purdey decided, however, that one particular rule had to be made express — even if it wasn't strictly necessary in light of his lordship's feudal powers of invitation. He drafted it as a defiant gesture in remembrance of Hector. It came to be called 'Purdey's rule'. It was a take on Macready's ever-changing 'Rule 19' and was similarly numbered:

19. For the avoidance of doubt, in construing these rules the masculine should be taken as meaning the masculine, however counter-intuitive that may seem. To put it another way, the masculine should *not* be taken as including the feminine. For those who have difficulty with the English language, "he" does not mean "she"; "him" does not mean "her"; "man" does not mean "woman"; and "gentleman" does not mean "lady".

It was naughty of Purdey, perhaps, (although Floodgate gave his blessing), to leak his 'Rule 19' parody to the Times diarist, who placed it prominently amongst the day's gossip on the morning of the grand opening of 'Hector's Club'.

And what a joyous occasion it was!

Hector's wines had been relocated to the cellars of the club bearing his name, and on this momentous night some found their way into the coffee room. Purdey, having accepted the burden of being chairman of the wine committee, dutifully tested a bottle of Château Margaux 2009. "It'll do," he said, as unashamedly happy as any Sandboy, Larry or Clam has ever been.

"It's like the old days," said General Sir Simeon Wallace-Black, pleased as Punch with his place at the head of the centre table—which Vivien Floodgate decreed should be reserved for him, not just that night but for all time.

"It's better," said Martin, marvelling at the collection of old masters indulgently spread over all four walls. Martin was at last a member of a club he frequented. The viscount, hearing of his history at Macready's, insisted he join Hector's simply as "Martin". From that day on, no one even tried to recall his surname, nor could anyone be bothered finding out if he really was a Roman Catholic priest or a glorious imposter.

The staff were as merry as the members, taking delight in remembering the names and titles of everyone, their preferences and their foibles. They had especially requested to have uniforms which exactly matched those they had been given in Macready's, and they wore them that night. Dr. Hans Fleischer, just a little tipsy, leaned back in his chair, beaming at the sight of them, and informed his bemused neighbour "I think I am experiencing a severe case of the psychological disorder Freud identified as *déjà vu*—Ya?"

If this were a movie, the camera would now pull back as though looking down from the chandeliers, with the whole contented scene bubbling below, smaller and smaller, until the laughter and the buzz of conversation were overtaken by music, and the to-ing and fro-ing of busy waiters had faded beneath the slow crawl of the end titles.

But this is not a film, and there is something more to be said.

There had only been one significant point of disagreement between James Purdey and Vivien Floodgate, and it concerned a cozy little area on the ground floor to the left of the main staircase, which seemed to Purdey ideal for a replica of Macready's 'broom cupboard'. It had a club fender for members to perch on and warm their backs in the winter; comfortable leather armchairs — the kind you can sleep in; and occasional tables for drinks and newspapers. But Vivien did not like the name 'broom cupboard' — he thought it belittling. He insisted, as he was entitled, that the area should be given the quaint name:

"Under the Stairs"

The End